DARK AND
BLOODY GROUND

The ranch had some kind of curse on it — all the owners had died violent deaths at the hands of unknown killers. Not even this would stop Tad Addison now that he had the chance to buy a place and start his own cattle empire. Addison was tough, but before it was all over, he would have to fight for every inch of that dark and bloody ground.

Books by Walt Coburn
in the Linford Western Library:

LAW RIDES THE RANGE

WALT COBURN

DARK AND BLOODY GROUND

Complete and Unabridged

LINFORD
Leicester

First published in the United States of America

Originally published as
'The Burnt Ranch'

First Linford Edition
published November 1992

British Library CIP Data

Coburn, Walt
   The dark and bloody ground.—Large print ed.—
Linford western library
I. Title II. Series
813.52 [F]

ISBN 0–7089–7257–8

Published by
F. A. Thorpe (Publishing) Ltd.
Anstey, Leicestershire

Set by Words & Graphics Ltd.
Anstey, Leicestershire
Printed and bound in Great Britain by
T. J. Press (Padstow) Ltd., Padstow, Cornwall

1

BRONC riding came natural to Tad Addison. That is what old R.T. Barnes told Tad's father. R.T. owned the Lazy B outfit and had a remuda of three hundred head of 'broke' horses besides two mare bunches and two of the best studs in Montana. The Lazy B ran cattle, but old R.T.'s hobby was raising good horses. And what there was that R.T. did not know about horses and handling horses had been torn out of the book.

Zack Addison, Tad's father, ran the livery barn in town and had a weakness for horse racing. He owned some trotting horses and two quarter horses that had been winning at the county fair and in matched races there in the little town of Black Coulee. Tad had broken every colt Zack owned.

Tad was about eighteen when R.T.

first took notice of him. Tad was breaking a three-year-old for his father. R.T. sat on the top log of the corral, along with a gathering of youngsters, town loafers, and half a dozen girls who openly admired the good-looking youngster who was handling the bronc.

R.T., after half an hour, climbed down from the corral and hunted up Zack Addison, who was playing pitch at the Deuce High.

"Zack, that boy of yourn is wastin' his time hangin' around yore barn. I'm hirin' him. He's a natural."

"Yuh mean, R.T., that you want Tad out at the Lazy B?"

"Tell him to come on out tomorrow."

"Dog-gone, now, I dunno about that. He's workin' with a promisin' three-year-old an' — "

"He kin bring the three-year-old with him. I got some colts ready to break. I'm paying the kid man's wages. Bronc-stomper's wages. Send him out in the mornin'."

That was R.T.'s way. He owned

most of the country, and his say-so went. Zack Addison nodded his bald head. He was a small man with a heavy reddish moustache and keen blue eyes.

"I'll miss the lad, R.T."

"Hire a man to take his place around the barn. Give the boy his chance. Cleanin' out stalls, fillin' mangers, and greasin' buggy wheels won't ever git him anywhere. If he makes good at my place, he's gittin' somewheres. And it will keep him outta the pool halls and work this town stuff outta his system."

★ ★ ★

And so Tad Addison began as bronc rider for the Lazy B. To Tad it was like a dream come true. To be sure, he missed his pool games and dances and the hero worship of the girls at school. But he was with men now — cowboys who worked hard and 'hoorawed' him and liked him.

There was a big bay bronc that threw him five times before he managed to ride the animal. R.T., sitting on the corral, said nothing. Tad's nose was swollen and bleeding. One leg was lame. His face was skinned. But he made no complaint, and not once did he fight the big bay bronc. And after he had ridden the sweaty horse around the corral a dozen times, he spat out dirt and blood from between bruised lips and grinned at his helper.

"Open the gate, Bill. We'll see what happens outside.

"Hadn't I better snub him to the saddle horn, kid?"

Tad shook his head. "I'll take him out as he is. Haze me away from the cut banks and wire fences, that's all." He settled himself in the saddle and slapped the bay's shoulder gently with his quirt.

Half an hour later Tad rode the big bay back into the corral. The horse was weary but not played out. No spur marks or quirt welts showed on its sweaty hide. Tad eased himself out of the saddle, hung to the hackamore rope as the big bay leaped sideways. He kept talking to the horse in a laughing, soft-toned voice. He unsaddled the bronc and slipped off the hackamore. Under the smear of blood and dust, Tad's face was grey with pain. He limped over to the pole corral, and with a grimy, bruised hand reached between the holes for the dipper in the bucket of water. The water was coated with dust, but the young bronc rider blew off the dust and drank thirstily. Not once had he seen his boss.

R.T., big, florid, lighted a fresh cigar. There were two more broncs to ride out. A wiry, line-backed buckskin and a wall-eyed, bald-faced black. He wondered what Tad would do. He grinned faintly as the youth kicked off his chaps and picked up his catch rope. Tad built a loop and opened the gate into the next corral, where the buckskin and bald-faced black trotted around, blowing hard through red-lined nostrils.

Tad roped the bald-faced black. With the aid of his helper he got the hackamore on the bronc. The saddling was a laborious, patience-trying half-hour.

"That bald-faced, wall-eyed son is goin' to break in two with yuh, kid," prophesied the hazer.

Tad grinned. "Snub him up close, Bill, and I'll climb him."

The bald-faced black 'broke in two' with a squeal. Tad put up a clean ride. He had lost his hat, and his curly black head was wet with sweat, powdered with yellow dust. His grey eyes were bloodshot. Perspiration ran in rivulets down his cheeks. His jaw was tight.

"Open the gate, Bill. Turn us out."

R.T. chewed on his cold cigar. He sat there until Tad rode the black back into the corral half an hour later. The youth slipped out of the saddle and talked softly to the bronc.

Tad took another drink of water that

was warm and not clean. Again he kicked off his chaps and picked up his catch rope. Again came that wearisome job of getting on the hackamore. The buckskin struck at the young bronc rider, and one flinty hoof tore away the front of Tad's shirt.

"First time I wore it, too, yuh fightin' rascal," Tad's temper was unruffled. Blood streaked his chest where the buckskin's hoof had ripped away the skin.

"Better call it a day, kid," said the hazer.

But Tad did not seem to hear.

★ ★ ★

Half a dozen times the bronc threw the saddle and blanket. It was sundown when Tad jerked the blindfold off the buckskin. Bill, the hazer, slacked the rope that held the bronc's front feet. The show was on.

The buckskin was a wicked pitcher. Limber-legged, always with a threat to turn over, it bawled and pitched. Tad lost a stirrup once and had to pull leather till he got it back. When he managed to pull the buckskin's head up, he grinned faintly.

"Thought for a minute I was goin' to stake out a claim. Open 'er up, Bill, and we'll take a joy ride."

Bill swung open the big pole gate without quitting the saddle. The wicked-pitching buckskin flashed past like a streak of yellow light. Bill spurred his horse to a run. The buckskin sank its head with a squeal. Tad rose loosely in the saddle. Half a dozen jumps, then it happened. Those limber legs under the twisting, sunfishing body gave way. There was a cloud of dust, a tangled jumble of horse and man as the buckskin turned over. Bill's tanned face showed white as he quit his running horse.

Now the buckskin lurching to its feet, pitching again, squealing, empty stirrups popping. Tad lay motionless there in the dust.

R.T. quit his perch and mounted his big brown pacer. When he got there, Tad was getting to his feet. He lurched forward a step, then stood there swaying — dirt, blood, rags, the Angora hair on his chaps smeared with dust. Tad pulled the back of his shaking hand across his mouth.

"Pick up the buckskin, Bill, and fetch him back," he said.

"You've had enough, young feller," said R.T. quietly.

Tad looked at him, then at his hazer.

"Fetch back that line-backed son, Bill."

And in the last light of the setting sun Tad rode the line-backed buckskin back into the corral.

★ ★ ★

In his log house that evening, R.T. Barnes looked across the table at his motherless daughter. Juanita Barnes was a leggy youngster of fifteen, with brown eyes and jet-black hair. She was just home from the convent at Great Falls.

"How did yuh like the bronc ridin', Nita?" And he laughed as the youngster's face went crimson.

"I saw you hiding in behind the branding chute," he went on, and behind his jovial manner was something as hard and cold as a frozen bit of whetted steel, 'watchin' Tad fan those broncs around. You're just a youngster, Juanita, but your mother was Spanish, and the women of her blood mature early. I've given you, and am going to give you, the education that is due the daughter of R.T. Barnes. I'm going into the senate this year. True, it's cattle and horses and free range that's putting me there. It's true that I was a cowboy and came to Montana with the first trail herds.

"When I'm talking to cowmen and cowboys, I talk their lingo. But when I'm in Helena, Senator R.T. Barnes, I'll talk their language — the language

I learned from books I bought when I punched cows for thirty dollars a month and beans. I educated myself. I studied books. I studied men. I studied horse raising, cattle raising. I own this county. I'm giving my daughter everything that a girl can want. Understand, Juanita?"

"Yes, dad. But I don't understand what you mean by first telling me that I hid in the branding chute and watched Tad ride, then talking about you being Senator Barnes."

The girl's brown eyes had a wistful, baffled sort of hunger in their brown depths. In a few more years Juanita would be as beautiful as her mother had been — her mother, daughter of one of the richest of Mexico's dons, who had run away one night with a gringo cowboy who took her up the cattle trail into Montana. Rumor claimed that the beautiful wife of R.T. Barnes had died of a broken heart. She had never understood the cold Montana country. Daughter of Mexico's music and flowers and laughter, she had been cowed by the stern pioneer folk who had come across the plains in their covered wagons.

And Juanita was the daughter of that woman of Mexico whose pride kept her from going back to her own people. And so she had died when Juanita was but a few days old. Her grave behind the ranch houses was marked by a marble headstone. And only the woman who died understood why she would have preferred a simple wooden cross and a grave in Mexico. R.T. had seen in her only her great beauty. He had never been capable of understanding the heart of the woman whom he had stolen from Mexico, no more than he would ever understand the daughter of that woman whom he had married.

"Juanita, never forget that you are the daughter of R.T. Barnes — Senator Barnes. Some day, United States Senator Barnes. Don't lose your head over a bronc-ridin' son of a no-account owner of a livery barn. When it comes time for you to marry, I'll find the right man for you. I don't mind you spending your vacation here on the ranch; but, if you are going to act the idiot on account of a bone-headed bronc rider, then I'll send you off to Europe with a chaperon. Is that plain?"

Juanita Barnes fought back the tears that threatened. She fought her anger against this father of hers who drank enough whisky in a day to kill the average man. She saw him now as a ruthless ruler of a cattle kingdom, a man whose lust for power was the ruling passion of his life. Juanita saw her father as few few people ever saw R.T. Barnes. There were times when she almost hated him, other times when she loved this man who had made of himself a power in a primitive land where only the strong can survive.

"I understand, dad."

"Good. Eat your soup before it gets cold."

R.T., supper over, was busy with his mail. So he did not notice Juanita slip down to the bunkhouse with liniment and bandages.

2

TAD was twenty when he rode Bad Medicine and won first money at the Miles City contest. R.T. won better than a thousand dollars on that ride. He had backed Tad. having a bronc rider like Tad Addison on the pay roll was not bad advertising for a man with political aspirations. The Lazy B outfit celebrated in Miles City that night. Next day R.T. had to bail out several of his cowboys who had helped paint the town red.

Tad was leaving for the ranch at daybreak the morning after the contest.

"I'm halter-breakin' ten broncs, R.T.," he explained, when his boss, meeting him at the barn, told him to stay over.

"Bill will take care of yore colts, Tad. Stay in town. Have a good time. It won't hurt you to take on a few drinks and shake a leg at the dance tonight."

He tried to hand Tad a hundred dollars, but the youth grinned and shook his head.

"I'm headin' for the ranch. Bill gets careless, sometimes, about waterin' and feedin' the broncs. It's plenty white of yuh, R.T., to ask me to stay and celebrate, and it's mighty white of yuh to want to stake me to spendin' money. But I don't have a taste for beer or whisky, and I don't take money I don't earn."

"If you pull out for the ranch and miss the barbecue and shindig tonight, you'll disappoint that good-lookin', red-headed waitress at the hotel. She's for you one hundred per cent. Have yore fun, Tad."

"I'd a heap rather go on to the home ranch, R.T."

R.T.'s voice lost a little of its bluff, jovial tone. R.T. usually had a motive behind every move he made.

"Better get this straight in yore head,

young feller: when a man works for me, he takes my orders. Whenever he gets too independent, he goes down the road talking to himself. You'll stay for the barbecue and the dance tonight or you're fired."

"Then I'm fired, R.T. I got all I want of this celebratin'. I ain't takin' that girl to the dance. I'm pullin' out for the ranch to go back to work with them broncs. If I'm fired, I'm fired." He threw his saddle on his top horse and ran the latigo through the cinch ring. Then he buckled on his chaps.

Senator R.T. Barnes took out his cheque book. "I hate to fire a good man, Tad; but when I give orders, I want 'em respected. How much have you coming?"

"About a hundred dollars. I don't keep track, much. The book-keeper at the ranch will know."

"Tell him to give you your time, when you get there. Looks to me like winning first money in the bronc ridin' has gone to yore head. I have no place at the Lazy B for a swell-headed cowboy that's hardly dry behind the ears."

Tad's jaw muscles tightened. It was with no little effort that he held his temper under control as the big, florid, loud-voiced owner of the Lazy B bawled him out. Yesterday R.T. had been loud and effusive in his praise of the Lazy B bronc rider who had ridden Bad Medicine. R.T. had put on quite a banquet in Tad's honor. And R.T. had gone to no little pains to make Tad acquainted with the good-looking, red-headed head waitress at the hotel.

Tad got into his saddle. R.T. stepped in front of his horse. The big cattleman forced a laugh.

"Perhaps I'm wrong, Tad. Every man is wrong sometimes. Forget what I said, son. It's a disappointment to me not to have you stay over. But I was anxious for you to have a good time. You don't get to town often, and all work and no play is not good for any man."

"No, sir. I know yo're plumb right. It's just that I got them colts tied up, and Bill is careless sometimes. I was lookin' after yore interests, that's all."

"Quite right, Tad, quite right. I wish there were more like you on the pay roll. Use your own judgment. I forgot to tell you I bought that Bad Medicine bucking horse. I'm entering him at the county rodeo next month. You'll win on him."

"But we have to draw for our broncs, R.T."

"I'll attend to that. So long, Tad. See you in a couple of weeks. And keep working on that black gelding. I want him gentled for Juanita. Surprise for her when she gets home next week from California. Have him lady-broke."

"He's gentle as a kitten, now. Even the Chink cook could climb on that Midnight horse from the Injun side and pack an open umbrella. He's a kitten."

Tad grinned widely, but R.T. had to

force a smile. Tad did not notice.

He was ten miles out of town when one of the Lazy B cowboys caught up with him. They rode along together. The cowboy occasionally drank from a bottle. Tad was rapped up in his own thoughts.

"Tad," said the cowboy, a grizzled range rider, "if I was you, I'd shore play my cards plenty careful."

"I don't know what yuh mean."

"It don't pay to cross a man like R.T."

"Who said I crossed him?"

"I was sleepin' off a jag there in the barn when you and him come in. I heard yuh talkin'."

"He saw things my way, at the end," said Tad. "Firin' a man for doin' his work is plumb foolish."

"Tad, yo're a good bronc rider. Yo're a good hand anywhere. But you don't see through R.T. a-tall."

"What do yuh mean by that?"

"R.T. is smart. He figgers things out. He studies every man he meets.

He had a reason for wantin' you to drink and sashay around with that red-headed gal."

"Shucks, feller, what reason would he have?"

"A big reason, young un."

"I don't git yuh."

"I know yuh don't, Tad. That's why I taken a wash in the water trough, got me a bottle, and rode out to ketch up with yuh. I wanted to give yuh some advice. You kin take it from a man that's worked for R.T. more than fifteen years. He's a bad enemy, boy. When he makes up his mind to git a man, he'll git him. And if you don't play his game, he'll git yuh."

"Why does he want to git me?"

"Juanita." The old cow puncher took another drink. "Juanita thinks yo're some feller. R.T. has other ideas concernin' that daughter o' his. He'd kill the cowboy that tried to make love to her."

"Shucks, man, Juanita is only a kid.

You been takin' the odd drink too many."

"Mebbyso. I didn't reckon yuh'd listen. Juanita is just a kid. But two years from now she won't be a kid. She'll be old enough to git married. She thinks a heap o' you, Tad. And R.T. knows it. That's why he wants you to drink and step around and mebbyso marry some gal like that redhead. Fact is, young un, he paid that redhead money to make up to you. One o' the boys heard him make the deal. She was to git you tight, then vamp yuh into marryin' her. But you didn't fall for the game."

"Gosh man, it sounds shore queer. I don't believe it."

"Go ahead and grin and laugh, but some day you'll find out I'm dead right. R.T. has a thinkin' head on top o' his bull neck. He kin think fu'ther ahead than any man I know. He missed fire this time. But he'll try again. He ain't used to bein' crossed. I never yet knowed a man that crossed him and didn't later on pay through the nose. If R.T. goes after yore scalp, he'll git it.

"Juanita is gittin' older every day. She's growed outta that long-legged awkward age. Before yuh know it, she'll be a woman. And R.T. will kill the cowboy that tries to make up to her. I've heard him say so. Tad, yo're the best bronc handler that ever set foot on the Lazy B Ranch. R.T. knows that. He wants to hang on to yuh. He aims to make a world's champion outta yuh — because it'll help him in his politics. It'll add to his glory to be able to say he owns the best horses and the best bronc rider in the country. It'll give him publicity. But, Tad, if you and Juanita git too friendly, yo're in for a heap o' hard luck."

3

AT the county fair Bad Medicine threw Tad Addison. R.T. lost fifteen hundred dollars thereby. R.T., in his private box with Juanita and some friends, among whom where Senator Lockhart and his son Bob, watched Tad's defeat. R.T. was a bad loser. He sat there, grim-lipped, his eyes narrowed to thin slits. He had watched Tad, out at the ranch, ride Bad Medicine time after time. Tad knew and anticipated every move that hard-pitching bucking horse could make. R.T. had somehow arranged the drawing of broncs so that Tad would get Bad Medicine. And now he sat there, boiling inside with red anger, as Tad was bucked off not twenty feet from the chute.

"Tough luck, R.T.," said Senator Lockhart, owner of the big Circle outfit. "Remember that old cow-country saying: "Never was a bronc that never got rode. Never was a bronc rider never got throwed." One thousand dollars you owe me."

The voice of the arena director came loudly: "Next rider Roy Long Knife from the Fort Belknap Reservation. Roy comes out of Chute No. 3 on Carrie Nation. Bob Lockhart wanted over at the chutes. Bob had drawed that twistin' snake named Cyanide. Too bad Tad Addison come apart from Bad Medicine. Citizens and foreigners, there was a bad horse throwed a good man. Bob Lockhart, git over here. Here comes that Assiniboine Sioux boy on Carrie Nation!"

Bob Lockhart, a well-built, handsome youth of twenty, just home from college, got to his feet. His father, a white-haired, aristocratic-looking man with white moustache and beard, smiled grimly and nodded.

"Have at it, son."

"Wishing me luck, Juanita?" Bob

Lockhart asked the girl who sat there, white-lipped, her eyes misty. Juanita had, in the past two years, become a young lady. Her beauty was almost breath-taking. She was watching Tad Addison, in overalls and an old flannel shirt, knocking the dust from his clothes with a battered hat. He limped a little, as he walked back to the chutes. There was a stoop to his square shoulders that was, to Juanita, eloquent.

"Wish me a happy landing, Nita?" repeated the blond-haired Bob.

"Of course, Bob." Juanita smiled faintly.

Her father scowled at her from under the brim of his bit Stetson. Only old John Lockhart, Bob's father, read the expression in her dark eyes. He patted one of her clenched hands and held it, unobserved by the others. Bob Lockhart left the box, his silver-mounted spurs jingling. A handsome, swaggering young cowboy was Bob Lockhart, and heir to several millions, for his father was rated as one of

Montana's wealthiest men.

"I'll be back in a little while," muttered R.T., and left the box.

He made his way across the arena to the chutes. Tad was behind the chutes, swabbing an ugly cut on his leg with raw iodine.

"Well?" growled R.T. "What's the excuse?"

"Excuse for what?" Tad looked up with a mirthless smile.

"You let that horse pile you. That's what I mean. A drunken sheep-herder could have put a better ride."

"Mebbyso. We'd just as well understand this business, R.T. That drawing was fixed. I drew a horse that I could ride bareback with my hands tied behind me and my eyes blindfolded. Sure I let myself get throwed. Not only that, R.T., but I've rode my last bronc for you. I'd sooner go back cleaning out stalls in my dad's livery barn. I'd rather grease buggy wheels. I'd rather be a barn boy than a crooked bronc rider. I've quit. Now get away from me, you big, bulldozing ox, or I'll bend a gun over yore fat head. I hope you lost yore socks on that ride."

"You — you — I'll get your hide for this, you young idiot! No man can talk to me like that."

"Dry up," said Tad quietly, his grey eyes cold with contempt and anger. "Dry up and get away from me. Send my check to Black Coulee in care of the barn. And don't hold out a five-cent nickel on me."

R.T. purpled. His heavy frame shook with rage as he took a step toward Tad, big fists clenched. Then he gave a gasp. His face took on a mottled, bluish hue. He dropped like an empty sack.

"Get a doctor!" called Tad. "R.T. just dropped down. Dead, mebby. Git a doctor!"

A few moments later Black Coulee's old doctor knelt beside R.T. He loosened the big man's collar. Somebody brought water. There was a swift hypodermic injection. And in a little while R.T. was sitting up.

"I've told you", said the little old country doctor, "that you have to take it easy. Too much whisky, that temper of yours, excitement — bad combination. May prove fatal some day."

R.T. got slowly to his feet. He glared at Tad, who stood there with a bucket of icewater. Tad stared back at him, no weakening in his steady grey gaze.

"I'll mail your check," said R.T. thickly, brushing the dust from his clothes. "Addison, I made you. Now I'm going to break you like I'd break a stick."

From the judge's stand the announcer was calling: "Roy Long Knife put up the best ride of the day. But get set for a thrill, cow folks and pilgrims, because here comes Bob Lockhart on Cyanide. And does that college-bred cowboy like his poison straight? Just watch him. There he goes!"

Bob Lockhart was making a pretty ride. As a matter of fact, he was putting up a spectacular ride on a horse that was not a mean bucker — a showy ride that had the grandstand cheering wildly. Handsome Bob Lockhart's white teeth were flashing in a grin, his white Angora chaps billowed with every jump. It looked like first money for Bob Lockhart as the timer's gun cracked and a pick-up man gathered Bob Lockhart and the bronc in.

In the judges' stand there was a whispered council. The three judges bent over a hastily scrawled note that bore the signature of Senator John Lockhart. The Senator and Juanita sat together in R.T.'s box.

The judges called in a swift parley. Then they called the announcer over to the stand. A moment later the announcer's voice cut through the other sounds.

"Ladies and gents: Tad Addison gets a re-ride. That ride he put up on Bad Medicine don't count. Tad will ride that notorious buckin' hoss called Mickey Finn. No man has ever qualified on that big roan man-killer. Know what a Mickey Finn is, folks?

It's a drink that knocks yuh colder'n a wedge, and before yuh go cold, yo're sicker than any ten men in the whole world. Tad Addison, git ready at Chute Number one for a re-ride!"

4

TAD grinned widely and hitched up his overalls. He wondered why they were giving him a re-ride. He hadn't asked for one. The bronc riders around him gave him rough, 'hoorawing' encouragement. He reckoned he needed it when he forked that Mickey Finn horse. He had seen the big, rawboned roan outlaw pile some of the best men in the rodeo game. He doubted his own ability to make a qualified ride. He'd never had a chance to study this Mickey Finn bronc. He picked up his contest saddle and started for Chute Number One. Bob Lockhart barred his way.

"So you put up a squawk to the judges, did yuh, Addison? Talked 'em into a re-ride, eh? You had one chance on a horse that you'd spent months practicing on. You got piled fair and square. Why don't you take your medicine like a man?"

"Well, if it ain't Purty Bob Lockhart!" Tad grinned, but his eyes were unsmiling. "All dressed up like a circus, givin' the ladies a big treat. Listen, feller, I never liked you from the time we were kids in the Black Coulee school. Every time you come back from that dude college, I like yuh less."

Tad dropped his saddle and doubled his fists. But other cowboys interfered and bustled Tad off to his bucking chute.

"I'll see yuh later", promised Tad, as they dragged him away.

"Any time, Addison. Re-ride Addison, the terror of Montana. That Mickey Finn horse will throw you back in the rear of the livery stable, where you came from."

Tad Addison was white with anger when he eased himself into the saddle.

"Give 'im to me", he growled, and was raking the big roan with both feet as they quit the bucking chute. The outlaw was squealing, bawling, pitching. Tad, white-lipped, was putting up the best ride he had ever made, fanning at the horse's sunken head with his battered Stetson.

An awed hush gripped the grandstand. Never had they seen such a wicked bucking horse. Never had they watched a better ride.

Danger there in every jump! This Mickey Finn was poison on a bronc rider because he was limber-legged. Every time he hit the ground, Tad thought the big roan would turn over. Twisting, bawling, sunfishing! And Tad, white teeth showing through the dust on his bronzed face, was making the only qualified ride ever made on Mickey Finn.

The timer almost forgot to keep his eye on the stopwatch. The three veteran judges watched in silence. Even the pick-up men forgot their duties in their absorbed interest. Every contest man knew that Tad Addison was riding as no man of them could ride, and they gave him the tribute of their rough approval.

In R.T.'s box, Juanita Barnes gripped the tanned hand of old Senator John Lockhart. She did not know that she was as white as chalk and that she was praying. Tears were wetting her eyes. And the white-haired old gentleman, with a rare understanding, held her tense hand in his.

Over in the bleachers, the cheaper seats, Zack Addison, dressed in his Sunday suit, sat with his cronies. He chewed one end of his drooping moustache, and his hands were clenched tightly.

The crack of the timer's gun sounded. Then it happened — a cloud of dust, confused glimpses of man and horse as the big roan turned over. A gasp of horror swept the grandstand. A woman screamed. The pick-up men came out of their stupor and spurred hard.

Now, across the arena, the big roan

outlaw tore, kicking and pitching. And through the dust could be seen the frantically struggling Tad Addison, one foot hung in the stirrup, being dragged, kicked at.

Old Zack Addison's face went grey. He put up a gnarled hand across his eyes.

The hush that gripped the grandstand was like the hush of death. Senator Lockhart was holding Juanita in his arms as she hid her face against his coat.

Across the open arena raced one man on a black horse — Bob Lockhart, ahead of the pick-up men. There was the splintering crash of wood as the stampeding roan hit the fence. And at the same moment Bob Lockhart quit his horse, flinging himself at the head of the roan outlaw. He was sitting on the roan's head when the pick-up men got there. They pulled the bleeding, unconscious Tad clear of the fighting horse.

Willing hands carried the broken,

apparently lifeless form of Tad Addison to the waiting ambulance. Bob Lockhart, his clothes torn and soiled, stepped up on his black horse. Bob Lockhart's cheek was ripped open from the bridge of his nose to the corner of his jaw. But he rode alone, at a lope, toward the chutes. Blood streamed from his face. He smiled as the applause from the stands reached him. Bob Lockhart loved applause. He had done a brave thing — done it skillfully. The acclaim of the crowd was his sweet reward. Up in the box, his father swore softly, albeit there was the gleam of pride in his eyes.

They took Tad Addison away in the ambulance. Zack Addison's friends helped the old barn man get there almost as soon as the ambulance reached Black Coulee's little hospital.

R.T. Barnes had gone to the town saloon.

The band struck up a tune. Senator Lockhart led Juanita from the box, and they were driven over to the hospital. It was typical of Bob Lockhart that he rode over on his black gelding and walked in alone to have stitches sewed in his face.

5

TAD ADDISON, bronc rider, did not die. But it was six months before he was out of the hospital. And, thanks to the best surgeons and orthopedic specialists, he was able to walk.

In its ignorance Black Coulee gave R.T. credit for spending the money that brought those specialists to the little cow town. And R.T., who was a good poker player, neither denied nor affirmed the rumor.

Old Zack Addison paid daily visits to the hospital. Zack, always smelling of the barn, and rye whisky, and pipe tobacco, Zack with his talk of horses that had broken records, Zack, basking in the mellow afterglow of his son's glory as a bronc rider — eager, always to tell friend or stranger of the ride that his son Tad had made on the outlaw horse called Mickey Finn. Zack, playing pitch at the Deuce High of an evening, boring friends, perhaps, with that often-told tale of Tad's greatest ride — recounting to anyone who cared to listen how R.T. himself had picked Tad for a 'natural' and had given the boy his big chance.

Zack was wont to get a little sentimental about Tad's start with R.T. Zack did not know about Tad's break with the big cattleman. Tad had not told. R.T. had not told. And if, in those long weeks when Tad lay in a hospital bed, old Zack put in more time at the Deuce High than he did at the livery barn no one blamed him. The life of a barn man is none too exciting. Tad's fame had lifted the little old man from drabness into a new world. He was now the father of one of the best bronc riders in the cow country. Tad Addison, his own boy, was the only man who had ever qualified on Mickey Finn.

Zack dug up a picture of Tad riding Bad Medicine. He got in touch with a photographer at Great Falls. The picture was enlarged and colored. Framed, it was hung behind the bar at the Deuce High.

Now and then R.T. dropped in at the Deuce High. With his customary bluff heartiness, R.T. would order drinks for the house. He would shake hands with Zack and treat him to a box of cigars. And Zack, carried off his feet by the friendly gesture of the great R.T. would sing the praises of Barnes in no small terms. This pleases R.T. in more ways than one. First, it got him votes and popularity. Secondly, it increased his contempt for Zack Addison and gave him another weapon with which to taunt the crippled bronc rider.

At the home ranch he would relate, with much detailed description, how the half-intoxicated father of Tad Addison was neglecting his barn to become little better than a bar-room bum, gleaning drinks and cigars from the oft-repeated tale of Tad Addison's ride on Mickey Finn. And R.T. took pains

41

that these anecdotes concerning Zack Addison reached the ears of Tad, lying in the hospital at Black Coulee.

As for Tad, he lay there, day after day, his body half cased in with plaster-of-Paris casts, the sun bronze gone from his face, hardly ever smiling. He asked no questions concerning the specialists who had made him well. He asked that no visitors be allowed. There were nights when the doctor had to use medicine to put him to sleep. And there were the black hours of night when Tad Addison lay awake, staring into the darkness, his body bathed with cold sweat, his hands clenched, his throat dry with choked-back sobs. And only Tad Addison and his God knew the suffering of the crippled bronc rider.

It was not pain that kept Tad Addison awake at night. It was not physical suffering that made him clench his jaws until his temples throbbed. It was something more fearful than mere pain. It was a terrible, stark flash of memory. The memory of dust and blood and shod hoofs kicking at him as he tried to jerk his foot out of the stirrup. Those brief seconds had grown into an eternity, that day. In a few split seconds, a few moments, he had felt the terrific horror that forever haunts the mind of a cowboy — being dragged to death, being kicked apart.

Tad's dreams were crammed with that red memory. He could not forget. He could not drive from his mind that awful moment that lasted forever, when he knew that his foot was caught — the never-to-be-forgotten thud of hoofs; the dust that choked him, blinded him; striking hoofs that struck his body, again and again — no pain; just the dull crack of his bones being smashed.

He wondered if that fear, that memory of fear, would be forever stamped on his face when they took off the thick bandages. Would that fear show in his eyes? So he told the nurses and doctors to let nobody but his father see him. He knew that old Zack was too proud of him to read anything like fear in his eyes. And so Zack, giving off the mingled aroma of livery barn, whisky, and pipe tobacco, would come each day and sit for an hour. And Tad would josh with the old man and swap stories of racehorses. And Tad's eyes would harden when his father lauded the virtues of R.T. Barnes.

And one day Tad Addison left the hospital, walking slowly, weakly, uncertainly. Refusing the help of an intern, he started out alone, on foot, for the livery barn and the little old cabin he called home.

A cowboy loped past. Tad halted, lips twitching, his eyes wide. The beat of hoofs had brought, in that split second, the memory, the red memory, of his last ride. After a little time he shuffled on with his cane. His face was drawn, tense, and his eyes were seared by a haunted stain of fear. The palms of his hands were moist, and there was a hard lump in his dry throat that felt like a hot pebble lodged there.

So Tad Addison returned to the livery barn. The barn was deserted save for the half-breed barn boy who was asleep in the saddle room. Tad went on to the little log cabin where he had been born and raised. The picket fence needed a coat of white paint. The gate hinges were rusty, giving out a dismal squeak. The flower-beds were filled with weeds. The little place carried the shabby cloak of neglect. But Zack Addison never was much of a hand for keeping things up. Horses were his life — horses and a friendly game of pitch at the Deuce High. That was all he cared for.

Tad went into the house. It smelled musty, a shut-up odor of stale tobacco-smoke and the faint aroma of the barn. Tad lifted the window shades and raised the windows to let in some air. Then he sat down on the old horsehair sofa and rested.

On the walls that needed new wall-paper were framed pictures of the different running and trotting horses

Zack had owned. Blue ribbons were pinned to the frames. There was a large, framed oval picture of Tad's dead mother, tinted and in a plain gilt frame, and also a smaller group picture of Zack, his wife, and little Tad in a velvet Lord Fauntleroy suit. Tad smiled at the memory of his hatred for that suit. Then he saw a large, framed picture of himself riding Bad Medicine. A dry sob choked his throat, and he buried his pain-twisted face in his hands. Hot, blinding tears wet his face.

It was nearing dusk when Tad Addison washed up and limped uptown to the Deuce High.

6

DAY after day Tad Addison lazed around the barn and corral. The sun tanned his face, and he gained back his strength.

"We won't be long now, son," said Zack, "till yo're knockin' on them Lazy B broncs once more."

Tad made no reply. Zack didn't notice. They sat on the top pole of the corral watching a bronc rider gentle a three-year-old. If Zack noticed any change in Tad, he never let on. And it is a certainty that Zack never guessed the tortures Tad suffered as he forced himself to sit up there and watch a horse throw a rider.

Night after night Tad Addison would jump awake from that eternal nightmare of being dragged to death.

"Feel like saddlin' one o' the gentle

uns and takin' a little ride, son? Do yuh good."

"Tomorrow, mebby. Not to-day, Dad."

He knew that Juanita Barnes had sent him flowers at the hospital. He knew that she had, without her father's knowledge, come to visit him and had been turned away. She was away at school now.

Rumors drifted into Black Coulee from the Lazy B and Circle outfits. Some of those rumors were ugly — stories of rustling, worked brands, stock run off. These rumors came from the smaller outfits who were losing cattle and horses. Tad listened in silence to these stories.

R.T. was in California for a few months. That meant that big Wayne Wallace was in charge. And Tad knew the ways of Wayne Wallace, who would do any sort of dirty work if R.T. told him to. Wayne Wallace was a Texan who was considered a bad man to cross.

Wayne Wallace came to town now and then. He was a big man in his thirties, with coarse black hair, black eyes, and the swaggering stride of a man who fears no one — a handsome brute, in a coarse way. His voice was a slow drawl, and he grinned a lot. But his eyes never smiled. He was as good a wagon boss as ever worked a crew of cowboys — and as treacherous as a snake. He had never liked Tad Addison.

"Back cleanin' out box stalls, Addison?" he had asked, grinning.

"There's worse jobs."

"Mebbyso. Grain my horse and don't feed him none o' that hay that's full o' foxtail. Heard the latest?"

"Mebby yes, mebby no."

"I was over at the Circle Ranch yesterday. Senator Lockhart's gone to California, an' Bob's celebratin'. He's got good cause to celebrate, I'll tell a man. Him and Juanita Barnes is gon' ti git married when she comes back from school. I bet that gives yuh a headache, hey, Mr. Bronc Twister?"

Wayne Wallace had swaggered up the street, silver-mounted spurs jingling. Tad sat a long time, there in the sun, whittling a stick, a queer look in his eyes.

After a time he quit whittling and walked up-town. He could walk now with only the trace of a limp. What Wayne Wallace had told him but confirmed the rumor he had heard several times. Marrying Juanita to Bob Lockhart would link the two biggest outfits in the country. It would mean power for R.T. Behind that engagement lay the clever, ruthless manipulation of R.T. Barnes.

Tad sought out a horse buyer who was at the hotel. They shook hands and talked aimlessly for some time. Then Tad broached his subject with characteristic bluntness.

"Who owns that Mickey Finn outlaw?"

"Don't know, for sure, Tad. He's pastured out with Bad Medicine and two, three more broncs that belong to R.T. Barnes."

"Buy him for me. Any price. Don't let anybody know who is buyin' him. I want that Mickey Finn bronc and I'm willin' to pay a top price. You'll git yore commission."

"Never mind the commission, Tad. You and Zack Addison ain't payin' me a dime. Not after the favor you've done me. If there's a way to get that Mickey Finn horse, I'll get him. But what do you want of a horse that come near killin' yuh?"

"Just a fool notion," said Tad.

And so it was that two days later Black Coulee learned that the big roan outlaw, now in the barn, belonged to Tad Addison.

No one was more astonished than Tad's father. Old Zack was agog with excitement. He wanted to ask Tad why he had paid a lot of money for a no-account, jug-headed, man-killing outlaw bronc. But something in Tad's manner forbade questioning.

At the Deuce High, old Zack chuckled and winked over his rye whisky. He assumed an air of mystery.

"Tad never said, men, but it looks to me like the boy's goin' to commence ridin' one o' these days. Yep. He sets there in the barn fer hours at a time, watchin' that Mickey Finn bronc. Like he's sorta studyin' out somethin'. Uh? Don't mind if I do. Another rye. And here's to my boy, Tad, the best bronc rider in the world."

The big roan had been delivered that morning. Tad had the cowboy who brought the bronc turn Mickey Finn into the corral. And Tad had sat there on the corral, hour after hour, watching the big roan outlaw. His face was grim, masklike. His eyes, under the slanted hat brim, were difficult to read because they were mere slits. The palms of his clenched hands were wet.

After a long time he took his catch rope and a hackamore. He roped the bronc and spent half an hour getting on the hackamore. Time after time he dodged the striking forefeet of the big roan. And in the end, when he had tied the outlaw in the barn, he had gone to the cabin and had lain there on the old horsehair sofa, his face grey and twitching, his body wringing wet with cold sweat.

7

OLD Zack played pitch until nearly midnight. He had taken on quite a few drinks and told some horse buyers, two shoe drummers, and a wool buyer about Tad's ride on Mickey Finn. This naturally called for more rounds of drinks. The portly, red-faced bartender afterwards said that he had never seen a happier human than old Zack Addison when Zack drank his final toast to his bronc-riding son and headed for home.

The half-breed barn man had found a bottle in a manger and had bedded down in the loft, dead to the world. It was Tad who found the broken body of his father next morning, there behind the stall where he had tied the big roan outlaw.

Tad carried the broken, lifeless body of his father into the cabin. It was sunrise, and the town still slept. Dry-eyed, his face drawn and grey, Tad washed the blood from his father's face and covered him with a sheet. Then he took his .45 and went to the barn.

The big roan was restless, nervous. Mickey Finn pulled back, reared, and threw himself several times. Tad, the gun in his hand, watched the bronc through slitted eyes. He stood in the next stall. He didn't know how long he stood there. He had come to kill the big roan outlaw. His brain was congested with milling thoughts. Self-reproach, hatred for the horse, sorrow and grief, twisted his thoughts into knots. He cocked the gun.

Then he slowly let down the hammer of the .45. He shoved the weapon into the waist band of his overalls and shook his head.

"I'll ride yuh some day," he muttered, his lips thin-pulled, bloodless, "and I'll drag it outta yuh. I'll ride yuh till yuh drop dead."

Then he quit the barn and went up the street to wake the coroner and doctor.

Next day they buried Zack Addison. Everybody in town attended the funeral. There were some who spoke about Tad Addison's lack of grief. Others whispered of Tad's folly in buying the roan outlaw, even going so far as to blame him for his father's death.

Perhaps, out of the crowd gathered there at Zack Addison's grave, one man alone understood. That man was Senator John Lockhart who had arrived that morning from California.

When the others had gone, when only Tad Addison stood there beside the open grave, old John Lockhart touched Tad's shoulder.

"Better come on home, son. Standin' here like that won't help. Zack's gone away."

He led the dazed Tad to his buggy, and they drove back to town. Senator John Lockhart went into the house with Tad. He poured Tad a stiff drink and made him swallow it.

"It — it was my fault, Senator. I — "

"Sit down, Tad. Don't keep broodin' like that. It wasn't your fault. Nobody with any sense thinks it is."

"But yuh don't savvy what I mean, sir."

"Perhaps I savvy better than you think, son. Now take off your coat and boots and lie down while I fix you another drink. Later on we'll go get some supper. Zack wouldn't want yuh to take it like this. Yuh know he was almighty proud of yuh, Tad."

"That's just it", said Tad through clenched teeth. "Dad was proud of me. He told 'em how great I was. Matter of fact I'm just a plain yellow — "

"Better swaller this quick before yuh bust down and beller. That's it. That's better. Now roll a smoke an' quiet down. I'm goin' to the barn for a little while. You get ready to come to supper with me."

Senator John Lockhart went to the

barn. He found the bleary-eyed half-breed barn man and for ten minutes shot short, brittle questions at him until the latter was whining and begging. John Lockhart's face was stern and hard.

"One word out of you about this," he finished, shaking his finger in the breed's face, "and I'll have you hung. Remember that."

Then Senator John Lockhart went back to the cabin and took Tad to the hotel where they had supper in the senator's room.

Tad was taking his father's death mighty hard. Zack had been more than a father to the motherless Tad whose mother had died when he was a smallboy. Tad had spent his spare hours hanging around the livery barn listening to Zack tell yarns or watching him work with his horses.

He forced himself to eat, there in old Senator John Lockhart's room. The older man talked about cattle and range conditions and the price of beef.

His kindness meant a lot to Tad just then. Tad thanked him and left after supper. He wanted to be alone. There were things he had to figure out. He walked to the edge of town and sat alone on the bank of the creek.

He reckoned he'd get rid of the barn. Staying there now meant torture for him. There were several men who would take the barn and horses off his hands at a fair price. He'd keep that Mickey Finn roan. And some day he'd ride that big outlaw till the horse dropped under him. The thought of stepping up on the bronc sickened him inside. He cursed himself for a yellow quitter.

Never before had Tad Addison ever thought of abusing a horse. But the big roan outlaw was to him a symbol of some sort — the symbol of his fear of a bronc. And the roan had killed his father, harmless, big-hearted Zack Addison who never in his life had abused a horse.

"I'll ride yuh, yuh roan devil!" he

said. "I'll ride yuh like no bronc ever got rode!"

He wandered back to the barn, drawn there by some strange emotion. The lantern was lighted, but there was no trace of the breed barn man. Now Tad pulled up with a quick gasp. Mickey Finn's stall was empty. The big roan outlaw was gone.

8

THE big roan outlaw was gone — stolen. All Tad could get out of the liquor-befuddled half-breed was that while he went up-town for supper, somebody had stolen the big roan. Tad shook him and slapped him and shoved his head in the water-trough, but that was all he could learn from the whisky-loving barn man. He finally gave up in disgust and went up-town to notify the sheriff. The first man he met was Bob Lockhart. Bob shoved out his hand.

"I'm sorry, Addison. I couldn't make it here in time for the funeral. Anything I can do?"

"Nothin', thanks."

Tad hadn't seen Bob since that day at the rodeo. They had told him how Bob Lockhart had probably saved his life by his fast action. He looked at the ragged scar that added to the handsomeness of the college-bred cowboy.

"I never got to thank yuh, Bob, for what yuh did that day."

"Forget it," said Bob. "Those pick-up men were too slow to catch anything that didn't crawl like a turtle. That Black Agate horse of mine can catch anything in the country except Midnight, Juanita's horse that I gave her. They're full brothers. Well, see you later, old man. Sorry about Zack. The barn won't seem the same without him."

Bob Lockhart went on. Tad saw him meet a girl who came out of the telephone office. He saw Bob kiss her, then the couple walked on, arm in arm, to be lost in the shadows of the night. Bob Lockhart's boast was that he could go with any girl he wanted to pick.

Tad found the sheriff at the hotel and reported the theft of the big roan outlaw. They had finished talking when a couple of men joined them — horsemen, friends of Zack. Less than an hour later Tad had sold them the barn and horses at a far better price than he had hoped for. He told them he thought they were paying too much.

"If we are, Tad, it'll be our first bad buy", they replied when they made out the check.

At the bank next morning, he learned that his father had left him twenty thousand dollars. That, together with the money he had got for the barn and horses, made a neat fortune.

"Any plans, Tad?" asked the banker.

"Not yet, sir. I'm all sorta mixed up yet."

"Drop around and see me when you get to feeling better. I have a proposition that should interest you. That is, if you'd care to pick up a ranch dirt cheap. It's a hundred-thousand-dollar layout, and I can let you have it for just half. One of the prettiest layouts in Montana. Horses, cattle, land, machinery. Lock, stock and barrel for fifty thousand dollars. You know the place. The Burnt Ranch.

It lies at the foot of the mountains on Rock Creek, next to the Lazy B range. The bank just took it over. R.T. tried to buy it not six months ago for a hundred and fifty thousand, but the owner wouldn't sell. As you know, we've handled the place for five years for the heirs of Rogers Curtis. An involved estate. Just settled. I'm giving you first chance at it."

"The Burnt Ranch", Tad spoke as if thinking aloud. "Rogers Curtis. He was murdered five years ago down in the badlands. I reckon yo're joshin' me about the price, though. The land alone is worth more than that."

"Precisely, Tad. I'd like to see you get it. Think it over and let me know as soon as possible."

"Yuh mean it, sir?" Tad, for the moment, forgot the big roan and Zack's death. The Burnt Ranch was a cowman's dream of paradise.

"I mean it, of course. Bankers don't make statements of that sort unless we mean what we say."

"Yuh done sold a ranch, sir." His face was flushed with eagerness.

"Good. I'll have the papers ready for you to sign this afternoon. Drop around at three. I'm making the terms easy. Ten thousand down and the balance in easy payments. Three o'clock, son."

Tad left the bank like a man walking in a dream. He hardly noticed where he was going as he headed for the cabin to pack up. In a few hours he would be owner of the Burnt Ranch. He could recall every log building on it; the corrals, sheds, bunk house and main ranch house; alfalfa fields; the mountains behind, the long panorama of rolling hills beyond — the crystal water of Rock Creek tumbling down the mountainside; the smell of pines and wild roses.

Then he recalled the sinister rumors about the place, from the Indian days when it had been burned out and the rancher and his family killed in their fight with the Indians. General Miles had his soldiers bury the dead. The graves were on a knoll behind the main ranch house.

Later it had been used by outlaws. Two notorious outlaws had been killed there in a fight with the sheriff's posse. Their graves were marked by granite boulders.

Then Rogers Curtis had bought the place and put a lot of money into developing it. He had come from the East somewhere. They said of him that he was too outspoken. He had openly branded R.T. as a cattle thief. He accused other cattlemen. He had made many bitter enemies. And one day his dead body had been found down in the bad lands. His grave, marked by a granite slab, was added to the other graves on the knoll. The mystery of his death had never been solved.

Tad dismissed these graves with a shrug of his wide shoulders. He had spent more than a few nights there and he had no fear of ghosts.

As he packed hurriedly, he tried to forget the grief that weighted his heart, tried to forget the fear of a horse that he must find and some day ride. And he tried not to remember that Juanita Barnes was going to marry Bob Lockhart.

While he was packing, old John Lockhart dropped in at the bank. The bank president invited him into the private office.

"Well?"

"I landed him, Senator. He don't suspect a thing."

"Good. As soon as he gets out there working, he'll come out of it in good shape. Tad Addison is the man for that ranch. He knows its history and isn't spooky. Besides, old Uncle Ben is there to wise him up. Tad Addison is goin' into a tough place, and his life won't be none too safe, but he has nerve and he's as honest a man as you can find. I need him and need him badly. Not a man workin' for me that I depend upon. Not even Bob. I'm hopin' Bob will get through sowin' his wild oats. He's scattered 'em from

Montana to New York. An expensive crop." He reached for his check book and a fountain pen.

"How much?"

"Fifty thousand. Tad Addison is costing you money, senator."

Senator John Lockhart chuckled. "If he wins out like I'm betting he will, he's cheap at twice the price. Now I'm getting off a wire to R.T. — a wire telling him that Tad Addison just bought the Burnt Ranch. I'm sending it collect and I'm signing it Wayne Wallace."

9

TAD, riding his pet rope horse, Big Enough, pulled up at the barn at the Burnt Ranch. At first he thought the place was deserted. Then, from inside the barn there came a man.

He was a small, leathery, little old man with a drooping white moustache. From under shaggy brows a pair of the brightest blue eyes Tad had ever seen, sized him up.

"You Tad Addison?" asked the little old cowpuncher in rusty boots, faded shirt, and warped overalls. Bent, bow-legged, he pulled a battered old hat across his eyes.

"I'm Tad Addison. Who are you?"

"I go with the place. I'm Uncle Ben. No use firin' me, for I go with the place. I'm as ornery a human as ever yuh sighted, and I git drunk twice a year — New Year's an' my birthday. After a spell yuh'll git so you don't pay me no attention. Git down, Tad Addison, an' put up yore hoss. Fetch any mail?"

"Just some newspapers, and a couple o' mail order catalogues, and a saddle catalogue, and one from a bootmaker." He untied the muslin sack from his saddle and handed it with its bulky contents to 'Uncle' Ben.

"No letters, Tad?"

"Nope. No letters."

"Ain't had a letter in forty years, but it never hurts to ask. I'll meet yuh at the house. Got a couple o' grouse to clean. How does grouse an' fried spuds an' sour-dough biscuits sound?"

The little old bow-legged cowpuncher cut a pigeon wing and chuckled. For the first time in days, Tad Addison grinned. He unsaddled and led his horse into the barn. As he cared for Big Enough, he wondered who this little old fellow might be. He had never seen him before, though he had stopped at the ranch several times. Nor had he ever seen the man in town. Tad thought he knew every man, woman, and child in that part of the cow country. Nor had it missed Tad's notice that the little old cowboy packed an old wooden-handled .45 in a worn holster tied to his thigh. Around his slim middle sagged a filled cartridge belt.

Tad kicked off his chaps and unbuckled his spurs. The fifty-mile ride had made him lame. It was the first he had ridden since his accident. He walked stiffly, limping a little. Uncle Ben met him on the big front porch of the log house.

"Set an' rest while I th'ow supper together, Tad. Take 'er easy. Nobody but you an' me here tonight. Hayin' crew is workin down on the lower place, and the three-four cowboys that ain't worth their salt is th'owing back some strays they gathered. Lazy B stuff that Wayne Wallace's smart cowhands tried to drift into our winter range. Young feller, do yuh know just what yuh bought into here?"

"I have a faint idea that it won't be any too soft. The Lazy B on one side and some other small outfits down in the badlands. Senator Lockhart's outfit on the east, but I'd trust his men anywheres. That's more than I kin say for the Lazy B outfit. I worked for R.T. and I savvy Wayne Wallace's brand."

"Then yuh know what I mean when I tell yuh that you don't ride alone nowheres and that we keep the window blinds drawed tight when we light the lamps. Don't forgit that bein' careless filled a grave up on the knoll that's marked with the name o' Rogers Curtis."

★ ★ ★

The supper and hot, black coffee made Tad feel like a new man. And after supper they sat out on the porch and smoked. Now and then Uncle Ben broke the silence with some little yarn that seemed to have entered his mind and needed voicing aloud. He talked like a man who has lived alone a lot and has a habit of talking to a horse or dog or some living thing. It was as if he were thinking aloud, and Tad wasn't obliged to listen or make any reply.

At first it was just a little annoying, but then he found himself listening to these broken anecdotes and after a bit he discovered that each one carried some scrap of knowledge that Uncle Ben wanted Tad to get. They were stories of the cow country, of this section of the cow country — stories of cowboys and of the outlaws who made their home in the badlands, stories of rustled cattle, stolen horses, shooting scrapes.

Darkness gathered, and still they sat there. Tad had little to say, and Uncle Ben broke a lengthy silence. "Mighty fine feller, Curtis. He had what they call ideals. Ideals about goin' straight an' honest and do unto thy neighbour as yuh'd like to be done by. Lots o' bone-headed cowpunchers thought he was loco. They couldn't ever savvy why a man in the cattle business never whittled on another man's cattle. They'd been brung up to think it was a disgrace to eat yore own beef. Swingin' a hungry loop was part o' their trade. And they called him a locoed fool. Called him harder names than that."

Uncle Ben stuffed his old pipe with cut plug and got it going. Then he went on:

"Rogers Curtis must 'a' knowed he was licked, but he was stubborn-headed that away. When a man fights fer money gain, he's likely to lay 'em down when he knows he's licked. But when a man fights fer these here ideals, he'll like as not keep on fightin' after he knows he's plumb licked. And that's what Rogers Curtis done.

"Some, like R.T., called him a coward because he didn't own a gun and wouldn't pack one. But the man that figgered Rogers Curtis a coward shore figgered wrong. He was an almighty brave man. And he died that a way. Though I reckon, in his heart, he kep' tellin' hisse'f that they wouldn't be low-down enough to shoot down a man that didn't wear a gun. He was like that. Always tryin' not to see the bad side of any man.

"But he died a-knowin' that he was wrong. And knowin' that his ideals about them men was all wrong hurt him more than the bullet in his back that killed him. He wanted to play the game on the square with them snakes. He played his game in the open. They played theirs from the brush. And while he suffered the torments o' hell that hour before he died, there in the badlands, he never whimpered once. All he kicked about was that he'd failed."

Tad wanted to ask Uncle Ben how he knew, but he did not. He knew that if Uncle Ben wanted him to know anything, he would tell him in his own way.

"I found him dyin', there along the

trail," the little old cowpuncher went on. "He'd stayed all night at my camp, the night before. And I'd tried to tell him that he was fightin' snakes, not men. We set up till nigh daylight, arguin' back an' forth. He'd trailed 'em down there. They'd run off some of his saddle horses. He wouldn't tell me who they was. He wouldn't tell me nothin' much. Just told me that he was goin' to have a show-down talk with 'em. When I wanted to go with him, he got almighty huffy.

"And the next evenin' I found him, shot in the back. They hadn't given him a chance. Nary a chance. No more chance than you'll git if they want yore scalp. No more chance then they'd give me if they suspicioned I know what I know. I done promised myse'f, that evenin' when Rogers Curtis died, that I'd live long enough to pay off that shot that they put in his back. And I will. Tad Addison, if you got good common horse sense, yuh'll go back to town and sell this outfit back to the bank."

"Why, Uncle Ben?" Tad smiled faintly in the darkness.

"Because yo're young an' yore whole life is ahead of yuh. Ownin' the Burnt Ranch is like a man holdin' a stick of dynamite with the fuse lit."

"It suits me," said Tad quietly.

"What if this place was sold to you because, we'll say, some outfit wanted a man here who had fight in him and was honest? What if you knowed you was just put in here to fight them cattle rustlers? Just a pawn in this game."

"I got the place cheap, dirt cheap," mused Tad. "I know there is somethin' behind it, from what you've said. But I'm takin' my chances. I own the Burnt Ranch. I'll fight to hold it. I know this country. I've heard talk. I worked for Wayne Wallace when he run the Lazy B round-up wagon over on this range and branded many a critter that belonged here. I savvy Wayne Wallace's connections with that maverick-stealin' gang down in the badlands. I'll fight for what I own. But I'll not make the mistake Rogers Curtis made. I'll pack a gun and I'll watch my step. I don't know you, and you don't know me. I'm askin' no questions, but I'm trustin' you from here on down the trail."

"It'll be a tough trail, Tad."

"All the better. I need a tough trail." Tad's voice sounded harsh.

"That's what John — that's the way I hoped yu'd take it, son. That's — Quick, Tad! Foller me! Around the back o' the house. And keep yore gun in yore hand!"

In back of some brush they crouched. A man rode up out of the darkness. They could see his blotted outline in the faint light of a new moon. The man whistled three times, a low-pitched whistle. From the brush Uncle Ben gave answer.

"It's just one o' the boys, Tad. He's a real hand. But whatever he is doin' comin' back here tonight, I don't know."

Uncle Ben hailed him, and the man

stepped off his horse.

"What fetches yuh here?" asked Uncle Ben.

"We was throwin' 'em Lazy B cattle back on their range, Ben. We was thrown' 'em back acrost the boundary about dusk. Some fellers opened up on us, and one o' the boys is hurt bad. he's at the old line camp on Rock Crick and needs a doctor."

"What was you boys doin' while they was shootin' at yuh?"

"Shootin' back as best we could. It was in a brushy canyon, and they was makin' targets outta us."

"Git ary of 'em?"

"I think I winged one gent as they drifted."

"Who was they?"

"It was dim light, and we couldn't tell. But there's only one cowboy in this country that rides a stockin'-legged, bald-faced black horse and wears white chaps and a white Stetson. He was one of 'em. He was givin' the orders, I reckon. Know who I mean?"

It was Tad Addison who spoke. "Bob Lockhart!"

The cowboy nodded. "It shore was Bob Lockhart. He was ridin' that Black Agate horse."

"When Bob Lockhart admits it," said Tad grimly, "I'll believe it. Not till then."

"Who are you, mister?"

"He's Tad Addison," said Uncle Ben quickly, for the cowboy's tone was hostile. "Tad's bought this outfit. We're workin' for him. Grab some grub and hit the trail fer town. There's fresh horses in the barn. Keep yore mouth shut about Bob Lockhart. Just fetch the doctor. I'll saddle yuh a fresh horse while yuh eat. Rattle yore hocks."

In the barn the little old cowpuncher faced Tad in the lantern light.

"If I was a fortune teller, Tad, I'd tell yuh that there's trouble ahead an' plenty of it. It'll be tougher than ary bronc yuh ever rode. A heap tougher."

Tad jerked the saddle from the cowboy's sweat-streaked horse and threw it on the gelding Uncle Ben led out of a stall. He grinned at the bow-legged little cowpuncher.

"Haze me clear of the cut banks and barb-wife fences, Uncle Ben, and I'll ride this Burnt Ranch business till I've gentled it."

"That's my job, Tad. Hazin' fer yuh. And I'm bettin' my other shirt that yuh make a clean ride."

The cowboy had bolted a quick meal and met them, there at the barn.

"Mind now," said Uncle Ben, "say nothin' to nobody. Yuh'll find a change o' horses at the same old places. Ride 'em like yuh owned 'em. Fetch that doctor. Good luck."

As the cowboy rode into the night, Uncle Ben started to blow out the lantern light. Tad stopped him.

"That bay horse looks stout, Uncle Ben, and fast."

"One o' the best in the remuda."

"I'm usin' him. I'll be back in the mornin' for breakfast."

Tad shook his head at Uncle Ben's

protests. He saddled the grain-fed bay horse. His grey eyes no longer were brooding. They were alight with the quest of excitement and adventure. He shoved his carbine into the saddle scabbard and grinned at the fuming, swearing, spluttering Uncle Ben.

"Wherever are yuh goin', any how? Ain't I wasted all evenin' tellin' yuh to be careful an' step easy?"

"I'm goin' for a ride, Uncle Ben. If I'm right, I'll tell yuh about it in the mornin'. But if I'm wrong, then we'll find Bob Lockhart and make him prove where he was this evenin' at dusk. If I have to beat it outta him with my fists. I bought the Burnt Ranch with its advantages and its ghosts. I'm laying them ghosts, and I'm startin' right now. I'll see yuh before noon tomorrow."

With Uncle Ben still spluttering, Tad Addison swung into the saddle.

The big bay was rollicky. It sank its head and pitched a few jumps, then was off at a long lope. The darkness hid Tad's face that was chalk-white, twisted with terror. He was hanging to the saddle horn so hard that his wrist ached. He was trembling, sick inside with that awful fear. It was half an hour before he loosened up in the saddle and rode easily. He headed for the Lazy B Ranch, riding hard.

10

IT was just before dawn when Tad hid his horse in some brush and went on afoot across the open space between the creek and the big barn at the Lazy B Ranch. He had taken off his spurs and made little noise as he slipped into the dark interior of the barn. He paused inside the barn, then made his way cautiously along the line of stalls. He talked in a soft undertone as he went, so as not to alarm the horses. Now he halted and groped at the fastening of a box stall. He called softly. In his hand was a large biscuit he had put in his pocket at the Burnt Ranch, just before he left.

A horse moved in the darkness and gave a soft nicker. Then Tad felt a velvety muzzle, lips nibbling at the cold biscuit.

"Yuh darned biscuit eater," said Tad

softly, and rubbed behind the horse's ears with an affectionate hand. Then he quickly passed his hands all over the horse. At last he risked lighting a match, then a second match. Now it was dark again. Tad rubbed the horse's nose for a time as the large soft lips nibbled his face and hair. Then he left the box stall and made his way toward the door.

"Stand where yuh are!" grated a harsh voice.

He saw two men outlined in the stable doorway — shapeless blots. He knew that he could not be seen in the darkness. That gave him the advantage. He notified the odor of whisky. He gathered himself, then dived at the nearer of the two men. The man went down with a grunt as Tad's gun barrel thudded against his head. The other man shot wildly as Tad mowed him down with a low tackle that would have done credit to a football player. Then he was racing for the brush.

Bullets snarled past him as he gained

the black shelter of the willows and swung into his saddle. He heard a man's shouted curses as he rode away. Men on horseback would be following him in a few minutes. He had been saving his horse for this reckless, hard bit of riding. He swung off the main trail, straight across country until he came to a barbed-wire fence. He fastened his rope to the top wire and took his dallies around the saddle horn. The wire snapped. The other four wires were broken in a like manner.

He rode through the gap, heading straight for the badlands. He forgot his weariness and the aching bones and muscles not yet hardened to the saddle. Confident now that he had slipped his pursuers, he swung off toward the Burnt Ranch. It was getting daylight, but the cut coulees were still in darkness. He kept to the coulees and draws that led out of the badlands, as he pushed on for the ranch.

In the half-light of coming day he picked out familiar landmarks. He was riding the twisted, almost trackless trail which Rogers Curtis had taken when he rode to meet death. Tad reckoned he was within half a mile or so of the spot where the rancher had been bushwhacked. He sat a little tighter in his saddle, and his hand was near his gun.

Suddenly he pulled up, listening. From somewhere in the near distance he could hear the bawling of cattle. Now, grazing cattle don't bawl. A herd being moved off the bed ground grazed without noise. But he heard the bawling of cows, the answering bawl of calves. It was too early in the fall for weaning calves, but Tads' cow sense told him that the racket he was hearing meant calves penned up somewhere and cows being driven away from those calves.

And this was on the border of the Burnt Ranch range where it joined the Lazy B. It was a broken, in some places, impassable, country — scrub pines, cut coulees, gyp springs, and soap holes that would bog a horse to its ears in half an hour; outlaw country where the cattle were wild; treacherous country that a man had to know by heart in order to cross, even in daylight. Luck had favoured Tad Addison in the darkness. But he wondered, as he slid the carbine from his saddle scabbard, just how long that luck would hold out. For he knew that he was on the verge of a grim discovery.

Cautiously, picking his trail through the broken country, he headed for the sound of bawling cattle. As he rode, he became aware of the fact that the bawling of the cows was decreasing. Mostly it was the calves that bawled now. That was odd. He shoved on in the dim light of daybreak, expecting he knew not what, except that he was riding into danger.

A miscalculation put him in at the head of a blind cut coulee — no trail, clay banks and shale fifty feet high. He turned back, swearing under his breath. He rimmed out below, his horse scrambling up a stiff slant on to a rim-rock ledge. From probably a quarter of a mile away he heard the din of bawling calves, and down yonder in that broken, timbered gulch, the half-angry, half-terrified bawling of a few cows. Then came the voices of men.

"One more fer yuh, Wayne — on the prod, too. Got 'er?"

Wayne Wallace's voice, harsh, commanding, replied: "Haze her in. Work fast an' earn that fancy pay yuh draw down. Prod her in, boys. And another critter takes a mud bath. That's it. Now fetch on the other two. Crowd 'em hard. Work, you curly wolves. You ain't got a sweat up since we started."

Tad got off his horse and squatted on the rimrock ledge, keeping himself and his horse out of sight. The bawling of the last cow ceased.

"All right, boys, let's go," Wayne Wallace's voice came up to him from the shadowy depths of the gulch that was choked with brush and scrub pine.

"We got them calves to move on. Let's git outta here."

From his vantage point Tad watched them ride up out of the gulch, single file — shadows of black against a grey sky. He let them ride away, then rode down into the gulch. He didn't know that there was a trail leading down there, and so let his wise cow-horse pick his own trail.

In the shadows of the gulch the horse stopped. There was a clearing about two hundred feet wide, a pole corral, and a chute. The chute was about twenty-five feet long. And at the end of that chute was a large pool of bubbling black mud, fifty feet across, its edges crusted with white. Where the chute sloped down to the mud, it was floored with hard pine boards. Prod poles leaned against the side of the chute. There was a huge bucket half filled with tallow and grease — grease that was used to make more smooth the slanting floor of the chute.

It was easy enough to figure out:

Weaned calves — cows herded into the pole corral and prodded down that slanted chute to the bottomless bog of the huge soap hole — cows killed there. To butcher an animal for meat was one thing — but this wanton killing of cows was akin to murder. White anger swept over Tad as he stared at those ugly bubbles on the slimy black surface. He'd ride to the ranch and get some men, then catch Wayne Wallace and his half-dozen rustlers. He'd —

"Lift'em high!" snarled a voice from behind some rocks and brush. "Plenty high, yuh spyin' fool!"

Tad tensed. His carbine was in his saddle scabbard. He could not make a try for his six-gun without getting shot in the back. He was trapped. He lifted his hands slowly. And in that moment he knew why Rogers Curtis had been murdered. Rogers Curtis had discovered this well-hidden spot where cows, perhaps men, were murdered.

There were two men in the brush. They talked to one another as Tad stood on the runway alongside the chute, his hands in the air, his back to his hidden enemies.

"Know him?" asked one of the unseen men.

"It's Tad Addison. yeah, I know him. And he knows me. That's why he's goin' into that bog hole after the cows. It's the pen fer me if he don't. Addison yo're covered. Make one funny move an' you'll git a hunk o' lead right where yore suspenders cross. Know who's tellin' it to yuh now?"

"I'd orter know. I've uncocked enough horses for yuh of a frosty mornin'. Taken the buck outta them crow-hoppin' cow ponies that you was scared of. Yep, I've let the hammer down on more than one horse you was scared to set on a chilly mornin'. I know yuh. Yo're that Circle rep they call Smitty. Still workin' for Lockhart, Mr. Man-Afraid-of-His Horses? Still drawin' Senator Lockhart's pay? Still ridin' Circle horses?"

"That's my business, Addison. You always was a little too smart to mix with common hands. Just smart enough, this mornin', to take what big Wayne calls a medical mud bath. Cures all pains an' troubles, Addison. I never did like yuh."

"That goes double, Smitty. A man that fights a horse would hit a woman. And a man that'd hit a woman would steal candy off a kid or kick the crutches out from under a cripple. I slapped yuh around once for fighting a horse. And so now I'm going to be shot in the back and slid down the chute? Well, Smitty, I'll —"

Tad made a backward, twisting leap and dived headlong into the brush. The two men were shooting wildly as he lay there on the ground, hidden by the dense brush. His gun was in his hand now. The brush moved, there beyond him, and he shot twice at the sound. A snarling groan told him he had hit his mark. He eased himself along the ground to the shelter of some rocks.

The brush moved, and he shot again.

"Don't shoot no more, Addison!" called 'Smitty'. "I'm shot up aplenty. Don't kill me! I was only foolin' yuh when I — "

Tad heard the roar of a gun off to his left. Smitty's voice died in a choked rattle. Now Tad was shooting toward where that murderous gun had barked Smitty's grisly death-warrant.

Bullets cut the brush around him as he lay prone, reloading his six-gun. Even as he ejected the last empty shell and shoved a cartridge into the chamber of the gun, the cracking of brush and swift pounding of hoofs told him that the other man had quit the fight and was spurring down the gulch. There was no advantage in following the man into a possible ambush.

He crept through the brush. Now, still crouched, his gun in his hand, he stared at the dead body of the cowboy called Smitty. Sluggish blood oozed from a bullet hole between Smitty's glazing, unshut eyes. Smitty had paid his price of outlawry. Killed by his own partner!

Tad found a saddled horse wearing the Circle brand, tied in some brush. He unsaddled the horse and jerked off the bridle. Then, covering the dead man with a saddle blanket, he got on his own horse and headed for the Burnt Ranch. The sun was rising in a grey sky streaked with red the color of blood.

11

AT the Burnt Ranch, Tad Addison found Uncle Ben in a bad humor. The old fellow met him with a sigh of relief followed by five minutes of swearing.

"Where in tarnation yuh been? Worryin' a man plumb off his feed. Yuh look like yuh'd tried to pet a wild cat. What yuh been up to, anyhow?"

That dive into the brush at the chute had scratched and lacerated Tad's face and torn his clothes. He was grey with weariness and the pain of his newly healed broken bones. His eyes were hollow, bloodshot. He grinned at old Uncle Ben's tirade as they went to the house. Tad saw a dozen saddled horses at the corral and a group of armed cowboys squatted around the barn. Some of them he recognized as being Burnt Ranch riders. Others were strangers.

Inside the house, Tad faced the little old cowpuncher. He pulled off his torn shirt and poured water into the wash-basin.

"Part of my trip netted me nothin' much, Uncle Ben. There's a horse at the Lazy B Ranch that's a dead ringer fer Bob Lockhart's black. I had a notion that some gent might be masqueradin' as Bob Lockhart. I checked up to see if that black horse belongin' to Juanita had been rode. He might 'a' been rode, but whoever rode him rubbed him down good and curried him off and brushed him. It was dark in the barn, and I didn't dare light the lantern. Which leaves Bob Lockhart more or less under suspicion. Though I'd bet all I got it wasn't Bob that was mixed up in that shootin'. I know Bob ain't a rustler. Shucks, why should he turn crooked?"

"There's a reason enough why Bob would go kinda astray, Tad. I know he's way in debt to R.T. Barnes, for one thing."

"In debt to R.T.?"

"About ten thousand dollars. A gamblin' debt that R.T. taken off Bob's hands. Never mind how I come to know, but I got the right information about it. Bob's a wild young un. Likes gamblin' and a good time. His dad has him on wages that ain't big enough to give him much rope. He loses to a tin-horn bunch that takes Bob's notes. When they threaten to go to the senator with them gamblin' notes, Bob gits desperate. he goes to R.T., knowin' R.T. is a hard gambler hisse'f. R.T. takes up them notes. Now mebbyso Bob Lockhart wants to pay off R.T., and he lets his foot slip. Bob Lockhart's a wild un."

"But he ain't a thief, Uncle Ben. I'd bet on it."

Uncle Ben looked hard at the young cowpuncher who was washing the dried blood from his face.

"You and Bob friends?"

"No. We never got along. Bob is the son of Senator John Lockhart. My father owned a little old two-bit livery barn. No, we ain't friends. Never will be, I reckon. But that's no reason for me to call him a rustler and a bushwhacker. And I ain't forgettin' that Bob Lockhart saved my life."

"You ain't pressin' no charges agin' him?"

"No. We'll do what we got to do without callin' in John Law. I'll handle it in my own way. Right now Bob Lockhart ain't so important, anyhow. Listen, Uncle Ben, I know now why Rogers Curtis was murdered."

"Yuh — what?"

Tad told the older man of his discovery down in the badlands and about the killing of Smitty.

"My bullet hit him in the shoulder, Uncle Ben. He started to beg. Started to weaken. His pardner killed him, then high-tailed it. I didn't dare trail him, because I knowed I'd run into an ambush. I recognized the killer's voice.

He's one o' the Lazy B tough hands. One o' that bunch Wayne Wallace fetched from Texas and Oklahoma. Smitty worked for Lockhart's outfit. That corral and chute have been built a long time. Five years or more. It's my notion Rogers Curtis stumbled on to it, and he was killed before he could tell anybody about it."

"Yo're wrong there, son. If he'd located that corral at the big soap hole, he'd 'a' told me before he died. But it's almighty likely that the fellers that was usin' that corral thought that Rogers Curtis had spotted it. I know he suspected there was a hidden weanin' pen somewheres in the brakes. He must 'a' rode close to where it is, and they figgered he'd located it. So they bushwhacked him. It must have been well hid. I've rode them hills over and across, backwards an' forwards, and I never found it. It explains away a lot. Rogers Curtis ain't the only man that got killed down there. But mostly they just disappeared. Tad, there's no use goin' down there after Smitty's body. It won't be there. By now it's in that boghole."

Tad nodded as he pulled on a clean shirt.

"And listen here. That killer feller is goin' to tell Wayne Wallace that you found that place. And if you go flyin' around the country alone, like yuh done last night, yore dead body will be dumped in there with Smitty's. I know yuh own this outfit; but, like I said, I go with it. I'm older'n you. I'm askin' yuh, Tad, to let me kinda ramrod the outfit for yuh and give yuh an old hand's advice when I figger yuh need it. How about it?

"It's a go with me, and I'm glad to take advice any day."

"I hoped yu'd see it that a way, Tad. Now go eat while I give the boys their orders. Git some grub into yuh, then take on some sleep."

"Where did those men come from, Uncle Ben? They ain't all cowboys that worked here the last time I was here."

"I done hired some new uns. Figgered we'd need 'em. There'll be plenty work for 'em to do."

"You bet there will," agreed Tad. "up till now the Burnt Ranch outfit never run a round-up wagon. They always had reps with other wagons. But next week we'll start with our own wagon and work our own range. And I'm sendin' word to the Lazy B outfit that any of their men ketched on my range will be run off as trespassers. They kin send a rep or two to work with the wagon and throw back all Lazy B stuff, but they ain't ridin' it between round-up. I'll tell R.T. Barnes why."

"How about Lockhart's riders?"

"I aim to take Senator Lockhart the same warnin'. Likewise, two-three other outfits down in the badlands. I got nothin' against Senator Lockhart, but there's some men like Smitty workin' for him that I don't want on my range. I'll ride on to town and explain it to him, personal.

And I reckon I'll do the same with R.T."

"Go git some grub, son. We'll talk 'er over later. The doctor's gone to the Rock Crick line camp, and they're goin' to try and fetch back that cowboy. The other boys is on the prod, and they'll need careful handlin'. They're ready to do battle with Wayne Wallace's outfit, and they want Bob Lockhart's hide hung on the fence. I got to calm 'em down."

* * *

Tad ate a hearty meal, then went into the front room of the big house where he and Uncle Ben stayed. He kept thinking of Bob Lockhart marrying Juanita Barnes. He reckoned she was in love with Bob. Bob was her kind. He had a good education, was of that handsome swaggering type that girls all fall for. Some day he'd own the big Circle outfit.

On the other hand, Bob Lockhart

would never remain true to any one girl. He bragged about his many conquests. And then there was his weakness for gambling and champagne parties. Tad's jaw muscles tightened. Before he'd let Bob Lockhart or any other man marry Juanita, he was going to plead his own case. He'd defy Bob Lockhart or R.T. or any other man to try to stop him. He'd write her a note and tell her about buying the Burnt Ranch. And he'd ask her when she expected to come home. He'd give Bob Lockhart a run for his money.

He opened the old-fashioned desk and pawed around for pen and ink and writing paper. Without meaning to do so, he picked up a typewritten letter, and half absently began to read it. Suddenly he stiffened. The typed words seemed to leap from the white paper at him.

— and I think Tad Addison is our man. Young Addison has courage and honesty and a level head. So

I fixed it at the bank so that the proposition was too good to turn down. He must not suspect that I had any part in it, understand. I trust your discretion and will need your help in handling him in the right way. Don't let him make any blunders. He's apt to be a little heady at times. We both know the risk and danger attached to this business. Hire what men you need to run the outfit. There is plenty of money at your disposal. And remember that young Addison can be handled with a hackamore, but never with a spade bit. Keep in touch with me as much as possible. Yours truly,

JOHN LOCKHART.

The letter was not dated and began 'Friend Ben'.

Tad sat there for a time, staring unseeingly at the letter. Something inside him had gone cold. That joy of fight to hold what he had bought, that thrilling pride of ownership of the

Burnt Ranch, had died inside him. No, he couldn't write that letter to Juanita now. He had no right to fight for her, because he had nothing to offer her. This ranch, which he had thought was his, did not belong to him. Tad's little interest in the Burnt Ranch was no better than a Mexican peso in a game where they used gold counters.

He was being used as a pawn in some game. He was little better off than he had been when he worked for his father at the barn. Worse off, he told himself bitterly. Now he understood about those high-priced surgeons who had attended him. Now he could understand that handsome offer for the barn, and that ridiculously low price he had paid for the Burnt Ranch. Senator John Lockhart was behind it all. It was politics of some kind, a deeper game than he could savvy. He was no better than a beggar, living on charity. Even old Uncle Ben was in on the deal.

Tad got to his feet, white-lipped with anger. He'd show this letter to Uncle

Ben and to John Lockhart. He'd make them come clean with the truth.

Then, half-way to the door, he checked his stride. He walked slowly back to the desk and tossed the letter in with the jumbled papers. He closed the desk and went to his bedroom. Every bone in his body was aching. He pulled off his boots and lay down on the bed to think. Then weariness exacted its price, and Tad Addison dropped off into a dreamless slumber.

12

DUSK was creeping into the room when Tad awoke with a start. He sat on the edge of the bed, blinking. He lighted the lamp and pulled on his boots. A hard, bitter smile tightened his lips as he remembered that letter. And with the remembrance of that letter he recalled his determination to play this game out to the last card. He'd keep his mouth shut and his eyes open. He'd play 'er out. He'd find out, before he was finished, just what it was all about. There was an old-fashioned, marble-topped washstand in one corner of the room, with a big white wash-bowl and pitcher and a clean towel. He was washing the sleep from his eyes when Uncle Ben's brittle voice hailed him from outside.

"Dang it, didn't I tell yuh don't

never light a light without first pullin' down the shades?"

Then, out there in the gathering dusk, Tad heard the clump of boot heels and jingle of spurs as the little old bow-legged cowpuncher moved away, chuckling and cursing to himself.

Tad pulled down the window shade and finished his hasty toilet. He joined Uncle Ben in the front room.

"I let yuh sleep, Tad, because I knowed you was tuckered out. The boys, some of 'em, is back. They done some snoopin' around down below in the badlands. Them weaned calves has been moved over on to the Lazy B range. They come on two, three head o' cows. Them cows had spikes drove in their hoofs to keep 'em from follerin'. Must 'a' bin fighting ol' cows that had broke from that soap-hole place an' aimed to foller their calves. What brand do yuh think they wore, son?"

The brand that belonged to the Burnt Ranch was Bench T.

"I reckon them was Bench T cows," said Tad.

"Nope. Each one o' them crippled cows was in Lockhart's Circle iron."

"Wayne Wallace is doin' business on a big scale, then. Whittlin' on Circle cattle ain't healthy. Let Wayne Wallace git caught and R.T. will quit him cold. And Lockhart's money will send him over the road for a long stretch. Wayne Wallace is dumber than I give him credit for."

"Don't be too plumb positive o' that, son. Fact is, he's somewhat a slicker hand than I had him figgered. Or else somebody smarter than him, some tricky cuss like R.T., might be puttin' notions in his head. We'll know in a few days."

"What do yuh mean, Uncle Ben?"

"Tad, that badland country is impossible to work clean, ain't it? There's bound to be calves left unbranded. you said you was goin' to run yore own round-up wagon this fall. You are goin' to send out certain word to R.T. and John Lockhart. They'll each send over some reps to work with yore wagon. It won't surprise me if Wayne Wallace reps for the Lazy B and Bob Lockhart reps for the Circle.

"Let 'em, then. I'll run my own wagon, and I'll send word to R.T. and to John Lockart that, after the work is done, they kin drift their cattle home, then stay beyond my boundaries." Tad's eyes were hard, his tone of voice harsh.

"Now, don't git hot under the collar, son. Wait till I finish talkin'. The boys left them crippled cows as they found 'em. Hard on the critters but it couldn't be helped. Now, young un, I'll bet you the best Stetson that money kin buy that by day after tomorrow, if a man rides down yonder, he'll find them three cows. The spikes will be pulled outta their hooves, but they'll be too sorefooted to travel far. And follerin' each one o' them Circle cows will be a fresh-branded calf a-wearing a big Bench T brand.

"Then, later on, when the round-up works through there, Wayne Wallace wills see to it that them Circle cows with Bench T calves will be picked up on circle and fetched into the hold-up. Bob Lockhart and the other Circle rep will see 'em. There'll mebbyso be more o' them cows in the Circle iron with calves that's wearin' yore Bench T. And you kin gamble on it that there'll be some Lazy B cows with Bench T calves a-follerin' 'em. Then there'll be more mammyless calves in yore iron. Weaned calves, mebby, but weaned two, three months too early.

"And, mister, it is goin' to take some tall explainin' to tell it convincin' about them cows and their Bench T calves. And more explainin' to account for them wind-bellied mammyless calves in yore iron. Then mebbyso Wayne Wallace an' Bob Lockhard will kinda, accidental-like, stumble on that corral and greased chute at the soap hole. Do yuh foller my drift, son?"

Tad nodded, scowling. He knew the

wisdom of all the older man was saying. It sounded possible enough. More than probable, in fact. Tad paced back and forth.

"Tad, they tell me that R.T. once told it at his ranch that he was some day goin' to hang yore hide on the fence. And from the way I look at it, he's makin' one shore purty try."

* * *

At supper Tad felt the uneasiness and tenseness of the men. Some of them he had known slightly. Half of them were strangers. They were silent-lipped, cold-eyed men who ate in silence, save for an occasional remark. Uncle Ben had little to say. Most of these men were older than Tad, and he had the notion that he was on trial. They were waiting to see what he would do, how he would handle this tough problem.

"Uncle Ben," said Tad, doing his best to make his voice sound casual, "How long will it take to get the mess wagon and bed wagon and the other stuff in shape to start work?"

"A week, anyhow. There's harness to mend, the tents to patch, horses to shoe. Takes time."

"Have some of the boys get at it in the morning. Fetch it in the remuda. Send to town for a blacksmith and whatever we need in the line of grub and so on. This outfit starts work a week from today. We'll work them badlands like they was never worked before. You boys will all be drawin' fightin' wages. If there's any man among yuh that feels like he can't fight for this outfit, he'd better draw his time tonight. From now on, you'll work plenty hard and you'll earn yore pay. I'll ramrod the outfit, and you'll take my orders. I won't ask any man to do anything I wouldn't tackle myself. If you got any holler comin', come to me with it. Unless yuh hired out for tough hands, you'd better draw yore pay and pull out for town."

Tad got up from the table and left

them sitting there in silence. He went down to the barn and saddled his horse. He was shoving his carbine into the saddle scabbard when Uncle Ben came in. Tad grinned faintly.

"If any of the boys want their time tonight, pay 'em off. Get things rollin' fast. I'll be back some time tomorrow night. If I ain't back, keep things movin', just the same as if I was here. Breakfast at three. Supper at dark. Gather in the remuda and figger out the strings of horses. Tell the cook to have his grub list ready by breakfast time. Start a wagon to town for what you need, first thing in the mornin'. Put a man down in the brakes to keen an eye on them three cows. Two men, if yuh ain't got one with enough nerve. Have yore nighthawk git busy and check up on his corral ropes and horse bells and whatever he needs. The horse jingler kin help him. Work 'em till they git so they'll learn to like it. If a man makes a holler, fire 'im. I'll be back when I git here."

"Hold on, hold on, son. Wherever do you think yo're goin'?"

"I'm goin' to see a gent named R.T. Barnes. Ever hear o' him? Then I'm lookin' up Senator Lockhart and his son Bob. I might likewise meet up with a snake named Wayne Wallace."

Uncle Ben's blue eyes puckered at the corners, there in the lantern light. He barred Tad's way.

"Aimin' to git yoreself killed, young un?" he asked.

"Not if I kin help it. But I ain't aimin' to take a lickin' layin' down. If its fight that R.T. is after, it's fight he'll get. And I'm aimin' to find out just where John Lockhart and his son Bob stand in the matter. Wayne Wallace has started somethin'."

"He has, son, fer a fact, an' if you go prancin' aroun' fool-headed, yuh won't be there to see the show-down. I tell yuh R.T. aims to git yuh. If you got a lick o'sense, yuh'll savvy what yo're up against. Goin' off half-cocked ain't winnin' yuh nothin'."

116

"Mebby not," said Tad, all the bitterness welling up inside him, "but R.T. is goin' to know he's not tackling a sheep-herder. I've tangled with R.T. before. And I've battled with Bob Lockhart since we was in the first grade together in school at Black Coulee. I don't know just what I'm up against, but I'm tellin' you this: that I'm fightin' this out and I'm lettin' 'em know just where I stand. Git outta the way, Uncle Ben. I'm travellin'."

Tad swung his mount past the little old bow-legged cowpuncher, and the fresh horse carried him into the darkness.

Uncle Ben stood there, swearing, but there was an odd twinkle in his puckered blue eyes. Perhaps something of Tad's headlong rush into danger was bringing back a part of his own youth — days when Dodge City and Tombstone were wild. For some time he stood there, staring out into the night. Then he headed for the bunk house at a trot. He called out a cowboy

117

from the lighted bunk house into the darkness.

"The young 'un has kicked over the traces. He's like a Injun on the warpath. I was scared he'd git that a way. He's tacklin' R.T. an' Wynne Wallace an' Bob Lockhart and gosh knows how many more. Buttin' his tough young head agin' a stone wall. He's liable to git killed. Trail him. Don't let him know it, but trail him. Keep him from doin' somethin' that will git him killed. Saddle the best horse in the barn an' stick with that hot-headed young bronc stomper like a sand bur to a blanket. But don't let him know. Keep in the background unless he gits in to a tight. Then use yore own judgment — and yore gun, if it comes to the worst. Now git goin'."

When the big, cold-eyed cowpuncher had ridden away into the night, Uncle Ben went to the house. He wanted to send a letter to John Lockhart. He sat down at the old-fashioned desk.

118

For a few moments, he searched through the papers and letters. Uncle Ben's disordered desk was not such a disorderly mess to him. He could always reach into the littered jumble of papers and find what he was looking for. And that letter which he now sought was not where it should be. It was not there at all. It was gone — that confidential letter from John Lockhart. Gone! And nobody but Tad Addison could have taken it.

Uncle Ben took a nip of rye whisky and water. He filled his old pipe but forgot to light it. It must have been an hour later when a rapping at the door aroused him from scowling thought.

"Who's there?" Uncle Ben turned down the lamp light and stepped to a shadowed corner.

"Open the fort, Ben," called a voice from outside.

Uncle Ben turned up the lamp wick and opened the door for Senator John Lockart.

13

TAD ADDISON reached town at noon the next day. He walked into the hotel and asked for R.T. Barnes.

"He's up in his room, Tad," said the hotel man. "How's the owner of the Burnt Ranch by now?"

"Can't kick none. What's R.T.'s room?"

"Number Five. Corner room on the front. Same one he's had for years. You know where it is."

"Anybody with him?"

"I think Wayne Wallace is up there."

"Good." Tad went up the wide stairs. He rapped at the door of No. 5, then walked in before he was invited. He stood in the doorway. His eyes, bloodshot from lack of rest, looked at R.T., who sat in a big armchair. Then his sidelong glance travelled to the bathroom door that was slightly ajar. Tad grinned faintly.

"Tell Wayne Wallace he needn't be hidin' in there, R.T."

R.T.'s red-veined face purpled. His narrowed eyes stared at Tad. Then he forced a short, blunt laugh.

"Come on out, Wayne. It's only our bronc-ridin' barn boy."

Wayne Wallace, looking as if he needed sleep, a stubble of whiskers on his heavy-jawed face, came into the room with a grin.

"Come in, Addison, and shut the door," said R.T. "Help yourself to a seat."

Tad closed the door and leaned back against it. "What I have to say, I'll tell it a-standin'."

"Suit yourself. Speak your piece, then get out. Wayne and I are busy."

"What I have to say," said Tad, his eyes hard, his voice low-pitched, more calm than he had hoped for, "won't take long. I just want to tell yuh that my round-up starts a week from now.

I'm runnin' it myself. I'll let you send over two reps. We're workin' the Burnt Ranch range clean. All stray stuff is bein' thrown off. And any Lazy B rider I ketch on my range after the work is done, I'll make a bunch quitter outta him. Is that plain enough for you both to savvy?"

R.T. looked at Wayne Wallace and grinned. "Hear what he said, didn't you, Wayne?"

"I ain't deaf, R.T."

"Addison," said R.T., lighting a thick cigar, "ain't you gettin' a little high and mighty? Wouldn't it be wise for you to sit down and have a drink and talk this over a little? You always were strong-headed, like a cold-jawed bronc. Supposing I told you that I had a good, fat proposition for you? Supposing we forget past quarrels and pull together? Wayne, take a walk down the street while I talk with this young man. I think there are a few things that can be settled without any further jangling."

"Stay where yuh are, Wayne," said

Tad. "What I got to say goes for you and the man that hires you to do his dirty work. Now git this straight before I go any fu'ther. I'm onto yore dirty game. Wayne Wallace knows that I got him where I — Keep your hand off that gun, you dirty cow thief, or I'll open up this jack pot with plenty aces." Tad's gun covered both men.

"R.T.," said Tad, as he read the expression on Wayne Wallace's face, "did this big cowpuncher of yours tell you I'd sighted him and his men at that corral at the soap hole? Did he tell yuh that I was there when Smitty was murdered by one o' yore tough cowboys? Did he tell you that I'm wise to the idea of tryin' to make me out a rustler by throwin' them poddie calves and them Lazy B and Circle cows on my range with Bench T calves follerin' 'em? Did he tell yuh that? Did he let you know he'd balled up his own game? How about it?"

R.T.'s red face was a study. The big cattleman's slitted eyes glared at the livid Wayne Wallace, then at Tad. Tad grinned faintly.

"I'll leave you two to talk it over, R.T. But, before I leave, just remember this: I'm — "

Tad had advanced a step or two into the room, his gun in his hand. Now that door behind him opened suddenly, and he heard a girl's voice, Juanita Barne's voice.

"Excuse me, dad. I didn't know you had visitors. Why, Tad! It's good to see you. But whatever are you doing with that gun?"

"Just showin' it to Wayne Wallace," said Tad, shoving the gun in its holster and taking her outstretched hand. Somehow, he didn't feel at all excited or flustered. He was self-composed, at ease, as he grinned down at Juanita, who smiled at him, a quizzical look in her dark eyes.

"Glad to see yuh back, Juanita," he said evenly.

"It's good to be back. And I heard that you are now a neighbour of ours

— a full-fledged cattleman. Are you going to invite me over to the Burnt Ranch, Tad?"

"You bet." Tad read something in her eyes that puzzled him. The last time he had seen her, she was more shy. Now she was acting like a grown woman — poised, sure of herself, unafraid. Tad wondered what had happened to the Juanita of a year ago.

"I got some business down the street, Juanita," he said, then added boldly: "I'd shore like to see you again before I leave town."

"Then we'll take in the show tonight. Street carnival in town. Calliope, pink, lemonade, popcorn balls, and peanuts to feed the monkeys and the baby elephant. They have one. And a wicked-looking little blonde ballet dancer. Call at the hotel at seven tonight, Tad. And we'll talk broncs between acts."

"That's a go, Juanita. So long, R.T. Remember what we talked about. Don't take any wooden dimes, Wayne."

Tad left the room abruptly, almost

bumping into a big broad-shouldered cowpuncher who was standing in the hallway. Tad looked hard at him, then grinned widely.

"I bet a hat Uncle Ben sent you to ride herd on me. Well, come along. We'll wash the dust out of our throats and take a look around town."

At the Deuce High, Tad bought the drinks for the house. The big cowboy who was called Joe had a fondness for whisky, and Tad took quick advantage of the big fellow's weakness. He knew that the cowboy had not eaten. He had been in the saddle since last night. It was hardly an hour later when Tad bedded down his bodyguard in a back room of the Deuce High and locked him in. Then he went up the street to the bank. But before he left the Deuce High, he called the grizzled bartender aside and slipped a ten-dollar bill in his hand.

"I'm obliged," he told the bartender, "for slippin' me the cold tea instead o' whisky."

"Shucks, Tad, don't mention it. I seen yuh ride into town, and right away I filled yore Old Crow bottle with cold tea, same as always. Tad, I ain't takin' this ten-spot — not from Zack Addison's son. Since you were knee-high to a hop toad, we've been pals. Many's the time I've sat there at the barn and told yuh Injun stories. I'm tellin' you somethin' now. Watch out. The Lazy B outfit is after yore hide. In my place, yo're safe. But watch out wherever you go. And not only that, Tad. Step into the office a minute, where we kin talk."

Inside the office the old bartender's voice dropped to a husky whisper. "Tad, that whisky-guzzlin' half-breed barn man that worked for yore dad has disappeared. And a good riddance o' bad rubbish. But before he up and disappeared, he was drinkin' heavy. Had him back in the snakeroom two, three times."

"The 'snake room' was where they laid out the drunks. Tad waited in silence while the portly saloon man got a black cigar lighted.

"That breed got the jimjams bad. Couldn't make much outta what he was jabberin' about, as he was mixin' up his Cree lingo with the little American talk he knowed. But, near as I kin figure, somebody was buyin' him whisky and keepin' him drunk. And Zack Addison wasn't alone when he come into the barn the night he got killed. And, between you and me, I doubt if it was that Mickey Finn bronc that killed yore dad. And if a man could git holt of that breed and make him talk, he'd learn somethin'."

"But the breed turned up missin' about the time I was goin' to have him slung in jail. Nobody's seen him since. Mebbyso I'm all wrong, Tad, but that half-Injun talked plenty queer when he was comin' outta them jags. Take it for what it's worth. And if you try to hand me any more money, I'll rap yuh with a bung starter."

Tad's grip of the heavy hand thanked

the big saloon man. Then he left the Deuce High and walked down the street to the little house where he had been born. He had not sold the house when he sold the barn. He unlocked the door and went inside, locking the door after him.

The place smelled musty, as shut-up houses do. Alone in the front room, he sat down on the old horsehair sofa to think.

His brain was crammed with jumbled thoughts — memories of boyhood; Zack's stories and jokes, often told, yet never uninteresting to the boy who loved him; R.T., bronc riding, Bad Medicine, Mickey Finn, and the fear that still clamped his heart in a terrific, icy grip; Juanita; Senator Lockhart's friendship that day of the funeral when Tad had needed a friend. It was hard to figure out Senator John Lockhart, and his son Bob who was going to marry Juanita. There was that Burnt Ranch deal — something big behind it all. Uncle Ben, who had told him much, yet held back so much more.

And the saloon man's warning and his strange talk about that half-breed! Who in the world would ever have wanted to kill the harmless, kindly-hearted, easy-going Zack Addison, who never had made an enemy? In Tad's mind everything seemed to date back to that day when R.T. had hired him to break broncs.

R.T. and Wayne Wallace, up there in Room 5 — when Tad had told it to 'em scary and made 'em listen at the end of a gun, how much had Juanita heard before she came in so abruptly? And why had she made that date with him tonight? Why had she changed so from that self-effacing attitude she had always had, into an outspoken young woman with eyes that warned him, pleaded with him, and encouraged him to say what he had to say to her, there with R.T. listening? And Juanita engaged to marry Bob Lockhart!

Alone in that little house so filled with many memories, Tad Addison tried to figure it all out; but the more he thought, the more confused things became. None of it made sense. The pieces of the puzzle would not fit. It was late in the afternoon when he remembered that he had not eaten. He shaved and took a bath and changed into clean clothes — a grey flannel shirt and a grey suit and his town boots, a new Stetson he had won riding broncs, a wine-coloured tie. After a beefsteak dinner at the Chink's, he felt like a new man. His .45 was shoved in the waistband of his trousers, hidden by his coat. It was still early, only six o'clock; an hour until he would meet Juanita.

At the hotel he asked for Senator Lockhart. The hotel man told him that Senator Lockhart was out of town. But Bob Lockhart was in town — up in his room. Just come in from the ranch. Did Tad want to see Bob Lockhart? No?

"I'll see Bob before the evening's over, I reckon," said Tad, and he grinned faintly to himself as he walked down the street to the Deuce High.

He saw Wayne Wallace and two Lazy B cowboys leaning against the bar. There were probably a dozen men in the place. A couple of card games were in progress. Tad went on through the bar-room and unlocked the door of the back room. The big cowboy from the Burnt Ranch was sitting on the edge of his cot, running his hands through his tangled mop of black hair. He looked sheepishly at Tad, who grinned.

"Feel better, cowboy?"

"If I felt much worse, Tad, yuh'd have to .order me a coffin. I shore went out just like Nellie's glass eye. And me promisin' Uncle Ben I'd ride herd on yuh. I'll git fired for this if he finds out."

"Are you workin' for Uncle Ben or are you workin' for me?" asked Tad bluntly.

"Why, dog-gone me if I ever — "

"Never mind. What was Ben's orders?"

"I was to trail yuh without you

knowin'. If you got into a fight, I was to stay with yuh to the finish." He got to his feet and grinned faintly. "I shore made a swell job of it. Ben will fire me, and I got it comin'. I smelled of a cork, an' passed out. The way my head feels, it'll take a size seventeen and a half hat to fit it."

"I jobbed yuh, cowboy. Uncle Ben won't ever know about it. We slipped you a little somethin' in yore drinks. That big Irish gent behind the bar will fix yuh up in two minutes. Yuh see, feller, I wanted to be alone for a little while. Had to do some thinkin'."

"Looky here, Tad," said the cowboy, pawing at his aching forehead. "I'm goin' to spill somethin' I shouldn't. R.T. is out to git yuh. He'll do it, too, if yuh ain't almighty smart. I heard what yuh called him an' Wayne Wallace in that room. I was listenin'. Then a lady comes along, and I had to walk on down the hall a ways. When she went in there, I come back. I still kep' on listenin'. Tad, are you aimin' to keep that there appointment with the lady?"

"I am, big feller, and I want you to quit trailin' me and keep an eye on Wayne Wallace. He's in the barroom now, tankin' up on red liquor. I'm slippin' out the back way. Git somethin' to clear yore head, then throw in with Wayne Wallace or else trail him. But don't trail me. I'm playin' my own hand. Got it straight?"

"I got it, all right, but I'm scared you'll git into a fight. I'd like to stay with yuh."

Tad shook his head. "Two's company, cowboy."

"And three's a fight if Bob Lockhart shows up."

"That's my business, cowboy. Takes orders or else quit."

"I'll take the orders."

Tad nodded and let himself out the door. He walked up the street to the hotel.

★ ★ ★

134

In the lobby sat half a dozen men. Tad's eyes took in the loungers there. At a far corner of the big, old-fashioned lobby, Bob Lockhart sat talking to R.T. They both saw Tad as he came in. Tad saw Bob Lockhart's face harden into a fighting mask. He saw R.T. shake his head and push Bob back into his chair. Tad walked over to where they were sitting and dropped into an empty chair. They eyed him coldly. Then Bob Lockhart's voice, low-pitched, tense, broke the silence.

"If I were you, Addison, I'd saddle up and quit town before I got into a lot of bad luck."

"And if I was you, Lockhart," said Tad evenly. "I'd lay off the hard stuff. Lemonade is a good drink. Bob, I was born and raised in Black Coulee. No man is goin' to tell me when to ride in or ride out. Sober up and I'll talk to yuh. There's a question I want to ask yuh."

"Ask it now, barn boy." Bob's bloodshot eyes glittered menacingly.

He had been drinking too much, and his voice was thick.

"I'll ask it when the sign is right, Bob, and for your sake and for the sake of your father's honor, you'd better have the right answer. I'm hopin' you have. And if you do have it, then we — "

"Why, you stable cleaner! You fool! You — *you* ask me questions? Listen, barn boy, and listen hard. Step outside and I'll beat a little sense into you. I've been wanting to do it for a long time. Step outside!"

Bob Lockhart's voice had raised. The men lounging in the lobby dropped their newspapers and watched. Bob Lockhart shook off R.T.'s restraining grip and leaped to his feet.

"Out in the alley, barn boy! Or are you too yellow?"

Tad's lips were bloodless now, and his voice was toneless when he spoke.

"All right, Bob. Outside. You're shore askin' for it. Let's git goin'."

Neither Tad nor Bob Lockhart or

any of the others save R.T. noticed the girl at the head of the stairs. As Tad and Bob Lockhart went out, followed by the excited lobby loungers, R.T. went up the stairs, two at a time. His face was mottled with anger.

"Back in your room, young lady. And this time I'm locking you in. Into your room!"

He grabbed her arms, pushed her down the corridor and shoved her into her room. He locked her in, then hastened back down the stairs and outside into the dimly lighted alleyway behind the hotel.

14

THE light in the alleyway was dim, but word of the fight had spread fast, and half a dozen lanterns glowed now. A crowd gathered. Tad shed his coat and handed it, with his six-gun, to the hotel man.

Bob Lockhart handed his gun to R.T., who was trying to get up some bets on the senator's son. Bob Lockhart was almost a cinch to win. Back at college he had been middleweight champion for four years. He was a fast boxer and a hard hitter. Tad's fighting ability was less scienced. Tad had experienced the average boy's share of fighting. And he had picked up something of the manly art of self-defense from a broken-down prize fighter who had worked for Zack at the barn one winter.

"Keep my gun, R.T.", Bob Lockhart

grinned. "It might be that the stable boy will want to finish it out with a smoke pole, so keep it handy for me."

"It'll be ready," said R.T., "but we don't want any gun play. Beat him up like he needs to be beaten. Gents, I have a thousand that says Bob Lockhart whips Tad Addison. Who wants any part of it?"

There were no takers. Tad and Bob peeled off their shirts. The crowd formed a circle.

"What rules, Bob?" asked Tad grimly.

"No rules. I'm comin' for you, barn boy."

Tad blocked a wicked swing and waded in. Bob covered as best he could as Tad's hard fists ripped through his defense. Tad was carrying the fight with a rush. He knew Bob's boxing skill. His one chance was to keep Bob off balance, rush him, batter down his defense, smash and tear through with jabs and hooks that would bewilder his more skilled antagonist.

Bob tried to clinch, but Tad hooked

him, sidestepped, swung a hard left to Bob's wind, then followed it with a terrific right that sent Bob reeling. Tad followed his advantage, raining blow after blow at Bob's bleeding face. Then he came into a clinch, hooking, jerking short, punishing jabs into Bob's mid-section.

They went down in a pile. Tad wrenched free, then caught Bob with a well-timed swing as the latter lunged at him. Bob reeled backward, off balance. Tad's second swing dropped him. Bob Lockhart lay there in a motionless heap. Blood oozed from his battered face, wetting the dirt.

Tad stood over him, breathing heavily. A hush held the crowd. Then Tad took his gun and coat from the hotel man.

"Lucky for you, R.T.," remarked some cowboy, "that nobody called that bet of yourn."

Tad shoved his way through the crowd. One of his eyes was swelling shut, and blood spattered his undershirt.

"Gosh, Tad," said a man, trying to

shake his hand, "that was a great battle. You sure cleaned Bob Lockhart."

Tad halted, shoving his six-gun into the waistband of his trousers. he was looking at R.T. when he spoke.

"Bob Lockhart was too drunk to fight. Sober, he could whip me easy. But he had to have a whippin', and I give it to him. R.T., you ribbed it. Now take care o' Bob. I'm goin' to the show up the street."

He went into the hotel and washed. R.T. and the hotel man had taken Bob Lockhart to his room. Tad's face was a little battered, and one eye was black and swollen almost shut. He put on his shirt and tie and coat and went into the lobby. It was a few minutes past seven. There was no sign of Juanita.

R.T. was up in Bob Lockhart's room. The hotel man was rushing up and down stairs with cracked ice and towels and ammonia and whisky. He looked grave and worried. Then the doctor came in, his black bag in his hand. He went upstairs. Tad sat in an armchair in a far corner of the lobby. His curt, almost surly scowl warded off the curious who sought to talk to him.

At seven-thirty, a small boy came in, looked around the lobby, then came over to Tad.

"Miss Barnes sent me, Tad. She's waitin' for you at the barn."

Tad gave the boy a dollar and finished his cigarette. Then he left the hotel by a side door and made his way down the street, keeping as much as possible to the shadows. She had changed her tailored dress for riding breeches and boots and a flannel shirt. She wore a buckskin jacket and a white Stetson.

"Dad locked me in, Tad, but I made a rope out the sheets and a blanket and made a regular prison get-away. I had to see you, Tad. Just had to. There's something I have to talk over with you. It's a question of life and death."

Tad grinned at her. "That bad, Juanita?"

"Just that bad, partner. But first, Tad, before we go further, did you and Bob fight over me?"

"Not exactly. Though I can't remember when we didn't fight over you. Bob had a drink too many under his belt and had his war paint on, that's all."

"You make a bad liar, Tad. That isn't all, and you know it. That's what we'll talk about later."

"At the tent show." Tad grinned.

"No. Let's take a ride. I feel — "

"Never mind how you feel," whispered Tad. "We're watched right now and we have to go careful. There's somebody hidin' back in the shadows. We're takin' in the tent show."

Tad's left hand gripped her right arm as they walked up the broad plank sidewalk. Soon they came within the lights of the tent show. They were lost in the crowd that gathered around the stands where the barkers ballyhooed the various concessions. Safe! Tad relaxed, and his grin became more natural. That burning spot between his shoulder-blades was gone. It takes a man better than a coward to walk through the shadows expecting a shot in the back.

"It was plumb foolish of yuh to meet me, Juanita," he told her as they went in with the crowd that was filling the tiers of board seats under the canvas top. "It's dangerous."

"I'm not afraid of danger, Tad. What I mean is, I am afraid, but fear can't count now. I — "

"Save it a while, Juanita. Let's git our seats — right here alongside the ring. Gosh, I like these shows! The smell of sawdust. The clowns. All of it. The crowds. Pop-corn balls and red lemonade. The baby elephant and the band playin'. It's about as close as a cowboy ever gits to grand opera. A barn-raised cowboy that — "

"Quit that, Tad." Juanita's voice was vibrant, no longer soft. "I knew that you'd grown bitter. Hard. Since that day when Mickey Finn almost killed you. I haven't seen you since that day. You wouldn't see me. Why?"

"Does it matter much?"

"It matters more than you know, Tad. It was like a knife cutting our friendship."

"I never meant it that way. Juanita, are you goin' to marry Bob Lockhart?" His voice was a husky whisper. The band was playing. The eyes of the crowd were on the circus performers.

Juanita groped for his hand. She found it clenched in a hard fist. She loosened his fingers and put her hand inside his — the hand that had knocked out Bob Lockhart.

"I'm not marrying anybody but the man I love. When I find the man I love, I'll marry him. Even if I have to run away and live in an Injun tepee. My mother ran away like that. She married my father — and died of a broken heart. No, I'm not marrying Bob Lockhart. Tad, I know what you want to ask me. I'm answering the unasked question. I'm being frank with you. I care for you a lot. Perhaps, inside my heart, I love you. And the man I love, I'll worship. But I could turn that love into hate if you ever harmed my father. Tad, promise not to hurt my father, ever. Will you do that for me? Your eyes tell me you love me. If you love me, you'll do that much for me."

Tad gripped her hand, then dropped it. He was thinking of his father now. He was trying once more to put together the broken bits of that strange puzzle. Zack Addison came first, genial, big-hearted Zack.

"I ain't makin' any promise, Juanita," he told her.

"Tad, I'll run away with you tonight. I'll go anywhere with you. I have all the money we need. Tad, please!"

"I'd just as soon kick a baby in the face as to hurt yuh," he said as his voice flattened into a monotone, "but I got a fight to make and ain't quittin'. I can't promise nobody on earth a thing. And yonder comes one reason why."

He nodded toward some cowboys who were coming in. In the lead strode Wayne Wallace.

15

WAYNE WALLACE was half-drunk — swaggering, spurs dragging, his hat pulled at an aggressive angle across one eye, his gun holster tied low on his thigh. Wayne Wallace was making it plain that he was tough and that he was on the prod. He had three or four of his men with him. They were tough-looking gun toters. As they took seats near Tad and Juanita, Wayne Wallace leered at them drunkenly and tipped his hat.

"The would-be bronc stomper shore fetched along protection," said Wayne Wallace. "He's smart, that a way."

His words carried up the row of seats to where Tad sat, tense as a coiled rattler, white-lipped with suppressed anger. The laughter of Wayne Wallace's cowboys made Tad flinch. He wanted to leap down over the seats and make

Wayne Wallace fight. His hand slid under his coat and gripped his gun.

"Don't Tad," whispered Juanita. "Wayne Wallace would like nothing better than for you to start a row. Then one of his gunmen would kill you. Don't let them prod you into making a gun play." She unobtrusively reached in under his coat and took hold of Tad's hand that was gripping his gun.

"Take it easy, cowboy," she said softly. "Don't let 'em make a fool out of you. Steady, pardner."

Something in the tone of her voice relaxed his taut nerves. He managed a sort of grin. The hand that had been gripping the butt of his six-gun now was holding Juanita's hand. She smiled at him, and he saw that she was pale and shaken.

"I don't want you killed, Tad."

"That bein' the case," said Tad, "I'll do my dog-gone best to stay livin'. Here comes the feller with the peanuts an' pop-corn balls an' red lemonade."

But Tad was not looking at the

man who was barking out his wares in a harsh, penetrating voice. He was watching two men who had come into the big tent. One of them was the big cowboy called Joe. And behind him came a smaller man, a little old bow-legged cowpuncher dressed in what the cowboys calls 'store clothes'. It was none other than Uncle Ben — Uncle Ben, with a bulge on his right flank where he packed his old .45 — Uncle Ben eating peanuts.

Uncle Ben and Joe picked seats near Tad and Juanita, blocking the way between Tad and Wayne Wallace. Apparently Uncle Ben was seeing nothing but the show down there in the sawdust ring. The brass band was playing a march. The performers were putting on their parade — spangles, sawdust, circus horses, clowns. Indians in war paint, a man in a big hat and buckskin who shot glass balls tossed by a cowgirl in fringed buckskin.

Uncle Ben looked back over his shoulder and telegraphed his message with puckered blue eyes. And Tad knew that the old cowboy was there on guard, that Uncle Ben's gun hand was ready. Tad grinned and reached into his pocket for money to buy peanuts and pop-corn and red lemonade.

Trapeze performers, tumblers, a milk-fed, roaring lion — then the big man in the white Stetson and buckskin, announced through a large megaphone:

"Laydees and gentlemen! Attention for one moment. Tonight we are putting on a special, an extra-special event. Through the courtesy of your fellow townsman and cattle king, Mr. R.T. Barnes, we have been able to procure the two greatest bucking horses in the entire world. The management offers a prize of one hundred dollars to the man who rides either of these two outlaws."

The band started up. From the rear of the big tent two cowboys in fancy show garb led a horse. Tad's face whitened a little.

"Laydees and gentlemen, the horse,

the great outlaw horse now being led into the arena is none other than that notorious bucking horse, Bad Medicine. One hundred dollars in green and yellow money to the cowboy that rides him according to contest rules. This is cow country, and I know that there are good riders in the audience. Who will take a chance?"

One of the cowboys with Wayne Wallace quit his seat. Tad knew the man to be a good bronc rider.

"Saddle yore bad Medicine outlaw!" he called, swaggering across the arena. "Give 'im to me."

The crowd cheered. The band started up again. Bad Medicine was snubbed to the saddle horn and front-footed and blindfolded. Tad watched, his jaw muscles like knots. The cowboy eased himself into the saddle. He lasted three jumps, then was thrown. Tad heard Wayne Wallace cursing the man for a drunken idiot because he had taken on too many drinks.

Another cowboy from the Circle tried Bad Medicine and was thrown. A third man tried the bronc and grabbed sawdust in two jumps. Bad Medicine was led out of the tent amid cheers and the noise of the brass band. Tad sat on the hard board seat, his hands gripping the board under him. Juanita was eating peanuts.

"And now, laydees and gentlemen, the boys are leading out the worst outlaw that ever throwed a bronc rider. Here he comes, folks! You are looking at that big roan man-killer, Mickey Finn. Five hundred dollars is offered to the bronc rider who can make a contest ride on Mickey Finn!"

"And a side bet of a thousand says no man here tonight can set that bronc!" bellowed Wayne Wallace, now on his feet, his hands full of banknotes. He looked up at Tad Addison.

Two men were leading the big roan outlaw around the arena. Something inside Tad Addison's heart was like a lump of frozen steel. That terrible, overpowering fear gripped him. Beads of sweat stood out on his tanned face. Juanita was saying something to him, but he could not hear her words.

Tad had got to his feet now. His face was a grey color. Like a man gripped by a nightmare, he made his way down the tier of seats and to the edge of the sawdust arena. Then a man's grasp was on his arm. He tried to shake it off. Other hands held him.

"Let me go!" he cried, trying to break free. "I'm calling that bet. That's my horse, and I'll ride him!"

He fought to get free. Dimly he heard Uncle Ben's voice. Wayne Wallace's harsh laughter. Tad fought now like a madman, blindly, without seeing anything but blurred faces. Not until he was outside and handcuffed and being taken away in the night did he come to his senses. The voice of the sheriff was telling him something.

"And it won't do any good to fight,

Addison. We've got you and we'll keep you."

"What am I arrested for?"

"Bob Lockhart is dying. And when he dies, it'll be murder. Get it, Addison? Murder!"

16

A CROWD surged around the sheriff, his deputy, and Tad. In the darkness, there in the flickering light of kerosene torches that lighted up the gaudy canvas posters of snake charmers, freaks, and the other circus attractions, Tad caught a swift glimpse of Wayne Wallace's sinister grin. He heard Juanita's frantic, hysterical sobbing, and R.T.'s growl as he shoved her clear of the mob. He saw Uncle Ben's blue eyes. Tad fought to get free. Then a gun barrel across his head brought oblivion.

The jail was an old log building that had once been a residence. The sheriff's office was the old front room. It had an obsolete fireplace and a worn Brussels carpet covered the pine-board floor. Beyond that were five rooms and the kitchen. The five rooms were guarded by barred doors. Iron bars were bolted into the window sills.

Tad's head was aching when he woke up in one of those rooms. He caught the odor of coffee and bacon that came from the kitchen. The cell room was dark. He was lying on a cot. The man in the next cellroom was probably drunk, because he was playing loudly on a harmonica, tune after tune — 'Turkey in the Straw', 'Little Brown Jug', 'Where the Silvery Colorado Wends Its Way'. And from the adjoining cell rooms other prisoners sang the half-forgotten words that went with the songs.

There was a lump on Tad's head, just above one ear. Blood oozed from it. He moved his arms and legs — dull pains but no bones broken. Now it was all coming back to him — the big roan outlaw; the fight to get there and ride Mickey Finn; the jumbled confusion; the memory of his fight with Bob Lockhart; the sheriff's words. Murder! Bob Lockhart! He hadn't hit

Bob Lockhart that hard. He'd just knocked him out, that was all. Murder?

It was hard for Tad to think clearly right now, because of that harmonica and the maudlin songs of the drunken cowboys locked in jail. But out of the jumble of confused thoughts came memories — Old Zack, Juanita, Senator John Lockhart who had befriended him when they had buried Zack that day.

He hadn't killed Bob Lockhart! Just knocked him out that was all.

And now Tad became aware of another sound — the gritty sound of a hacksaw biting its way through steel.

Tad got to his feet and went to the window. It was dark outside. But a hacksaw was cutting away the steel bars, outside the glass of the window. He thought he could make out a man's face, a hand warning him back to his bunk.

The harmonica and the tipsy singing were drowning out the noise of that hacksaw. The big cowboy called Joe played the harmonica.

Tad could look out of his cell-room and up the old hall into the sheriff's office. A deputy sat in an old-fashioned armchair with a cigar in his mouth and a magazine. The night was a little chilly, and there was a fire going in the old grate. There was a partially empty bottle of whisky and the remains of the steak dinner on the table in the office. Tad watched the magazine slide from the deputy's hands, saw the deputy's head tip forward in slumber.

Now came a gentle tapping at the window. Tad raised the window cautiously. The bars were sawn away. A hand motioned him. Tad nodded.

Making as little noise as possible, Tad crawled through the window and out into the darkness. He paused to close the window behind him.

"Rattle yore hocks, Tad," whispered a voice.

"Ben!" gasped Tad. "Uncle Ben!"

"Who'd yuh think it was, yuh young

bone-head? Think it was the mayor er R.T.?"

"Is Bob — "

"Dunno," old Uncle Ben cut in testily. "Come along. Git goin'. This is a jail break, not a sewin' bee."

Beyond the jail, in a brush patch, was a saddled horse. Uncle Ben handed Tad a six-gun.

"Don't use it till yuh have to, Tad."

"But listen, Uncle Ben. I got to see Bob Lockhart. I got to see Bob's father. I ain't runnin' off like a coyote."

"You ain't seein' nobody. Yo're headin' for the badlands, hear me? An' I'm givin' yuh orders right now. You ride that horse till he takes yuh to that old trapper's cabin on Seven Mile. I'll meet yuh there in a night or two — soon as I git news. Keep hid in the badlands of a daytime. Hang around in the brush near that cabin at night. I'll git there, quick as I git news how Bob Lockhart is. If he dies, you'll have to quit the country."

"I never killed Bob Lockhart. I never

hit him hard enough to hurt him."

"Who said yuh did, yuh young bone-head? Bob Lockhart's skull is fractured bad. It was done with a gun. It was done *after* the fight he had with you. And if I ain't badly mistook, it was done by the same murderin' son that killed Zack Addison. Now hit the trail!"

The music of the harmonica and the tipsy singing came to them as Tad gripped the gnarled hand of Uncle Ben. Old Ben chuckled.

"I filled that jail plumb full o' Burnt Ranch cowboys. And the bartender at the Deuce High slipped a few drops into the deputy's bottle. Now ride along, Tad, an' don't worry. And I'll keep yuh posted."

"Just one thing, Uncle Ben. You tell Senator Lockhart that I never did that to Bob. Tell him — "

"Git goin', Tad. This ain't no time to auger like two cowboys on day herd."

"Looky yonder, Uncle Ben. See what

I see? Look at that mob comin'. So that's what the game is. A necktie party, is it? Uncle Ben, you high-tail it. I'm standin' my ground. Wayne Wallace can't make a bunch quitter outta me. You drag it for home, Ben. I'll handle Wayne Wallace and his herd o' skunks."

"Yuh bone-head!" muttered old Uncle Ben, as he picked a sawn-off shotgun from its hiding-place in the bush. "I always heard that bronc riders got loco after a few broncs had shook away their brains. Now I know it to be the truth. Well, if yo're bound to make a fool outta yorese'f, all I kin do is back yore play. We're two agin' fifty. Yuh shore do pick nice odds when yuh play."

"I ain't runnin' from any lynchin' bee," said Tad.

"Yo're a young idiot. Clear out, won't yuh?"

"Run away from Wayne Wallace? No, Uncle Ben. No kin do. Now you slide out while there's time."

"No kin do, bone-head. Joe an the boys is inside — "

"So I figgered, Uncle Ben. An' I'd be lower down than a snake's belly if I run for it. Let's go!"

17

"STAND yore hands!" Tad's voice ripped through the darkness like a saw. He and Uncle Ben crouched there in the darkness as the mob headed by Wayne Wallace charged the jail door with an improvised battering ram made of a corral pole. Others in the mob had kerosene torches they had taken from the carnival outfit.

The dozen men with the battering ram halted. One of the mob yelped in agony as Tad's shot tore the flaming torch from his hand. The kerosene torch on its long stick fell to the ground. Its flame set fire to the drying grass.

"Let 'er burn!" shouted Wayne Wallace hoarsely. "Burn the jail! We've been double-crossed. Burn down the jail. Addison's in there. The dirty murderin' snake! Burn down the jail. It's full o' Burnt Ranch men, anyhow. Set 'er afire!"

Uncle Ben had put down his sawn-off shotgun and now thumbed back the hammer of his old cedar-handled six-gun.

Once, twice, and a third time he shot with the rapidity of an automatic.

"Take off yore hat, Wayne Wallace," he called out, "and count three bullet holes in it. The next bullet will ketch yuh plumb where them eyebrows o' yourn meet. Git back, yuh murderin' sons, or there'll be some killin'."

Inside the jail the deputy was gathering his muddled thoughts. The prisoners were quiet now. Every man of them had a gun that had been slipped in somehow by Uncle Ben. Locked in their cells, they were ready to make a fight. Big Joe called to the deputy. As the deputy came down the hallway of what had been an old reside, half a dozen guns covered him.

"Unlock these celldoors," commanded

165

Joe. "Make 'er fast, mister, because us boys is kinda impatient. Nobody's burnin' us to death. Hurry, yuh thick-headed sheep-herder. Unlock these cell doors or I'll shoot the ears off yore head."

The deputy obeyed the orders given by the cold-eyed grim-lipped cowboy. Joe slapped him on the back.

"Good work, feller. Yuh won't lose nothin' by this. Nothin' but a few prisoners in jail for bein' kinda disorderly up-town."

"Where's — where's Tad Addison?" gasped the deputy.

"Out there where the stars shine like diamonds in the sky and where the air smells fresh an' clean. Never mind Tad. Now throw down on them jaspers outside an' tell 'em that us boys ain't in the right frame o' mind to be roasted alive."

But even as he spoke, the flames were licking at the door and windows. Once the fire caught, the log building would be an inferno.

Outside, guns barked. Wayne Wallace was roaring orders. The mob, composed of Wayne Wallace's gunmen and hoodlums from the carnival, were half-drunk and reckless. They were being paid for this night's grisly work. Many of them had blackened their faces to disguise themselves. They shouted and jeered and sang songs as the jail caught fire.

Now, into that firelight, into the mob, there rode half a dozen armed men — the buckskin-clad show owner on his big white horse; some cowboys; Senator John Lockhart astride a borrowed horse; the sheriff and two deputies beside him.

"Back, you drunken fools!" barked the tall showman, a gun in each hand. "Back to the tent, you rubes! Clear out of this mess or I'll open up on you, and there's real cartridges in these old guns. back to the lot, you drunken roustabouts!"

For many months, and in many places, those carnival roustabouts and hangers-on had obeyed the word of that tall, broad-shouldered, white-mained man in buckskin. They faded away, melting into the shadows of the night. Senator John Lockhart rode his horse up to Wayne Wallace.

"Tell your men to fight out that fire, and do it fast."

"I take my orders from R.T. Barnes," Wayne Wallace sneered.

"Then get ready to take 'em," snapped Senator John Lockhart, "because here he comes."

R.T.'s face was a red mask. He bellowed orders colored with profanity. Wayne Wallace and the Lazy B cowhands sullenly obeyed. With water-soaked blankets they whipped out the flames.

When the fire was out, the sheriff unlocked the jail door. He and R.T. and Senator Lockhart went inside.

All was in order. The prisoners were back in their cells. But there was no sign of the deputy who acted as jailer. And the sawn bars of Tad Addison's cell told their silent story.

"Addison's escaped!" roared R.T., whirling on the sheriff. "What's the meaning of it? That young killer has escaped."

"And there's a deputy missing." The sheriff scowled. He faced the prisoners in their cells. Big Joe was once more playing his harmonica.

"Where's the jailer?" snapped the worried sheriff.

"Jailer? What jailer, sheriff?" Joe said, then resumed his harmonica playing.

The other cowboys began singing. The lights in the jail were dim, and so it was that neither the sheriff nor R.T. saw the gagged and bound figure of the deputy who was stowed away under Joe's bunk. That same lack of light hid the faint smile on the drawn face of Senator John Lockhart who left the jail and went back to the hotel where his son lay between life and death.

Near the hotel he met Uncle Ben. The old cowpuncher nodded and grinned faintly in answer to the questioning look in the eyes of Senator John Lockhart.

Tad, riding a stout, grain-fed horse, pushed hard for the badlands. Still dizzy with bewilderment, he attempted to make sense of it all, then gave it up and tried not to think.

Back in town the sheriff was organizing a posse to follow Tad Addison. Out in the street, there in the dim lights and black shadows, the mounted men gathered. Wayne Wallace and his men were in the posse. Back in the blackest shadows big Joe and his cowboys sat their horses. The jail now held but one occupant — an irate jailer who tugged laboriously at the ropes that bound him.

One man rode alone into the night, ahead of the posse. That man was old Uncle Ben. He was headed for the Burnt Ranch. The grizzled little cowpuncher rode hard for home. He would change horses three times between town and the ranch. He whistled tunelessly through his teeth as he stood in the stirrups and gave his horse its head. Had there been any light, it would have shown a grim smile on his leathery face, though his blue eyes were as hard and cold as deep ice.

18

THE trapper's cabin on Seven Mile, down in the badlands, was a place shrouded in mystery. For the most part of the year it was deserted. Now and then smoke came from the old rock chimney. Few men had ever seen or talked to the eccentric old trapper who had made the cabin his home for the past five or six years. The white-bearded trapper, with his long white hair, shunned all white men, so it was said.

He got his supplies through the Indians who came and went and were always welcome. There were tales about a lost mine that he was hunting for. The storekeepers in town showed nuggets that the Indians brought in to pay for the grub and tobacco and clothing wanted by the old trapper. They called him the loco trapper. He had a habit of running off all visitors with a shotgun or rifle. He never spoke, using only the Indian sign language or other crude ways of hand talk. No man knew his name.

Tad, as he neared the cabin in the badlands, recalled the different tales woven around this loco trapper who paid for the supplies with gold dust and nuggets. Most of those tales were undoubtedly the product of some cowboy's fertile imagination.

But this much was half-proved fact: The loco trapper had known Rogers Curtis. There were books gathering dust, there in the old trunk in the cabin, that had the name of Rogers Curtis on the flyleaf. And it had even been told that the loco trapper was an ex-convict, escaped from somewhere, and a relative of Rogers Curtis, who had been murdered near there. Another story was that the man was an escaped lunatic.

Tad had seen him several times — a hunched-over old man whose face was covered with a matted white beard, whose gun had warned Tad away; a man whose attitude was that of one who wants to see no other man, talk to no other man. And more than one man who had come near that lonely cabin had been sent back with a bullet snarling past his head.

Tad wondered why Uncle Ben had sent him to the cabin of the loco trapper. What if the old man were there? He'd run Tad off with a gun.

Tad felt relieved when, a little past dusk the day after his escape from jail, he rode up to the old log cabin and found it deserted. No smoke came from the rock chimney. The sign showed that no man had been here recently. He unsaddled and hobbled his horse and went inside. He had not eaten since the day before. Tad had heard that the loco trapper always kept food in the cabin — canned stuff, flour and beans and coffee.

Inside the cabin it was almost dark. A ray of dim light entered the cabin from the door Tad opened. That grey light threw a long rectangle across the dirt floor of the dark cabin. Save for that uncertain bit of light the cabin was dark.

Then, outside in the dusk of the badlands, came the nicker of a horse. Tad's horse gave answer. Tad shut the door with his left hand. His right hand gripped his six-gun. There in the darkness, he crouched near the closed door. An uncanny feeling had gripped him like the clammy hand of death.

There was something wrong, here at this deserted cabin — something dangerous, sinister, like the stab of a steel blade in the dark. He knew that he was not alone here in the darkness. He held his breath, listening. From somewhere in the blackness of the cabin came the uneven, labored breathing of a man.

"Strike a match," growled Tad, "or I'll commence shootin'. Light a match so I kin see just who yuh are."

"Don't shoot. I'm dyin'."

There followed a scratching sound, and a match flared. For a moment, the light of the match flickered, then went out. But in that brief moment Tad had seen enough.

Tad lighted a candle and bent over the bloody, broken man on the bunk. In spite of the beard and the blood and dirt Tad recognized the injured man as the half-breed who had worked for Zack at the livery barn — 'Cree' Antoine, whose love for a whisky bottle amounted to a disease. Cree Antoine was dying. He had been shot half a dozen times. He reeked of bad whisky.

Tad lighted a fire in the little camp stove and put on water to heat. He cut away the breed's shirt and undershirt.

"Who shot yuh, Antoine?"

But he could get only a mumbled reply from the dying man. Tad found the half-breed's half-emptied jug and poured the man a drink. The harsh liquor revived the wounded Antoine somewhat.

"Me, I'm talk too much, mebby. Them fellers find out, mebby, 'bout that talk. More whisky. Me, I'm die."

Tad gave him another drink. Death was already greying the half-breed's face. The bloodshot eyes were dimming.

"Talk about what, Antoine?" asked Tad tensely. "Talk, man."

"Bout dat night when dey keel Zack, yore ol' man. That horse, she don' keel Zack. Like I'm tell John Lockhart de trut' 'bout how them two fellers knock Zack hon de head, when Zack tell them fellers 'bout bad talk he hear 'em make 'bout you. Me, I'm tell John Lockhart 'bout that. Then Wayne Wallace give me some money han a bottle han tell me to steal de horse han go to the ranch.

"So I'm steal de Mickey Finn horse han one more horse han lead dat bronc to the Lazy B Ranch. Cowboy there give me more money han de jug han tell me to quit de country. Dat night me, I'm get dronk. I'm sit by de fire han smoke de pipe han sing planty.

Like de wolf sing. I'm get purty dronk. Somebody shoot me drom de brush. Shoot me hin de back. but I'm not die there. I'm get hon de horse han ride away hin de night. Me, Antoine, know 'bout this place. I'm come here to die inside de cabin where de wolves han de coyotes don't get me. Me, Antoine, I'm — die."

Tad tried to force whisky down the rattling throat. He worked frantically, desperately.

"Who killed my father, Antoine? Who murdered Zack Addison?" he cried hoarsely.

But there would never come any reply from the open lips of the half-breed. Cree Antoine was dead.

19

TAD found Antoine's horse and uncinched the bloody saddle, then turned the animal loose. He hid the saddle in some brush. He was in no position to notify the sheriff of Cree Antoine's killing. He would have to let that dead body stay in the cabin. There was an old tarp on the bunk with which he could cover the body. But even as he opened the door of the cabin and went inside, the scurrying of rats in the darkness made him shudder.

He lighted the candle and prepared the bullet-torn body for burial, wrapping it in the old tarp. He found a short-handled shovel such as a trapper carries on his saddle to dig out coyote dens. And outside in the darkness Tad began his grim task of digging a grave. There was a white moon that shed a ghostly light through the scrub pines. An owl hooted dismally. Back in the hills a wolf sang its song to the white stars.

The ground was clay, and Tad had to use the axe to get through the hard-packed crust. He was weary from the long ride he had made, every muscle was sore, every nerve rubbed raw. He needed sleep and rest and warm food. But he labored on, there in the white light of the moon, digging a grave for Cree Antoine, who had carried the secret of Zack Addison's death with him.

But, no. Tad's weary brain was remembering now. Antoine said, when he was dying, that he had been murdered because he had talked too much to Senator John Lockhart. Then John Lockhart must have the key to the mystery. John Lockhart knew who killed Tad's father. Why, then, had John Lockhart been so secretive about it? Was he shielding someone? His own son, for instance?

Sweat bathed Tad's body as he

labored with the shovel, digging deeper the grave that was to hold Cree Antoine. He reckoned that the hole was deep enough now. He put aside his shovel and stooped to lift the tarp-wrapped body of the dead man.

A bullet whined over him. A man's harsh voice called from the black shadows.

"Raise 'em high, Addison! And what's more, keep 'em high."

Tad straightened slowly. He raised his arms in the air. He had recognized the hidden voice as belonging to the sheriff.

Half a dozen men surrounded him. Handcuffs were snapped around his wrists. He was led back to the cabin and shoved inside. Then some men brought in the tarp-wrapped body of Cree Antoine.

★ ★ ★

Tad faced them, there in the candlelight. The dead man was laid out on the bunk. In the posse were several Lazy B cowboys, a man from the Circle outfit, and the harmonica-playing Joe. Joe caught Tad's glance and winked. The sheriff looked up quickly from his examination of the dead half-breed.

"Looks bad for you, Addison. Understand, whatever you say kin be used against you. But there's some questions that'll bear answerin'. Might help you to tell the truth."

Tad forced a faint grin. "Sorry, sheriff, but I ain't talkin'. Take me to see Senator John Lockhart. I'll talk to him. I was aimin' to head for town, directly I'd planted Cree Antoine. I got to see John Lockhart. I got to see him quick before more murder is done."

"We'll see John Lockhart when we git to town, young feller. Don't worry about missin' him. But we ain't startin' back just yet. There's been murder done here, Tad, whatever made you kill Cree Antoine?"

"Figger it out for yoreself, sheriff, if you think I did the killin'. I'll ask you one. How'd you locate me here?"

"You left a plain trail. A sheep-herder sighted you headed this way. We spread out. Struck a blood trail just about sundown, and it came this way."

"Who found that blood trail? Antoine's trail?" asked Tad.

"Wayne Wallace found it. We're waitin' for Wayne right now."

"Supposin', sheriff, that one of the boys builds up a pot of coffee and some grub. I could use it. Last meal I had is so long back I've forgotten what it tasted like. So it was Wayne Wallace that located the blood trail, there where Antoine was shot? Smart feller, Wayne Wallace. Handy kind of a gent to have around, ain't he? He's shore a top hand at settin' fire to jails and pickin' up blood trails. Sheriff, we should have R.T. Barnes here. Then the party would be almost complete."

"What do you mean, Addison?"

"Nothin'. I got a habit o' thinkin' out loud sometimes. Just like I got a habit o' rememberin' things. Cowboys usually have good memories. They remember brands and earmarks and so on. Sorta trains a man's memory. And that's how come I remember somethin' my dad told me. Remember my dad? His name was Zack Addison, and he run a livery barn in Black Coulee. Remember Zack Addison?" Tad's voice was low-pitched, drawling.

"Look here, Tad, are yuh drunk? I knowed Zack for years, and you know it. My house ain't a five minutes' walk from the barn. What are yuh tryin' to say, anyhow? What's that got to do with you killin' Cree Antoine?"

"Rememberin' brands and ear-marks," Tad went on, rolling a cigarette with his manacled hands, "kinda trains a man's memory. I was in the barn one evenin' about feedin' time, curryin' off a horse. R.T. Barnes come in, and you was with him. R.T. had a bottle. It was just before election time. You didn't see me because I was in the box stall curryin' a horse. R.T. pulled the bottle, and you all had a drink — a drink to the election, a drink to the next sheriff.

"Zack Addison drank with you and R.T. Then R.T. mentioned somethin' about how dad could swing a lot o' votes at election time and how there'd be a case o' whisky an' a keg o' beer on tap here at the barn. And how the voters should vote for you to be the new sheriff. And yuh tried to hand my dad some money. It was one of the few times I ever seen my dad git on the prod. He told R.T. to take his money and clear out. And he told you that he wouldn't vote for you if you was the last man on earth. And he told you and R.T. to git out of the barn before he run you out with a pitchfork.

"R.T.'s money elected you, and you know it. Just as well as you know R.T. hates my insides. And now R.T.'s paid killer is tryin' to hang this murder on me. Wayne Wallace is framin' this deal. Find the man that killed my father. Find the man that knocked Bob Lockhart on the head up in the hotel room. Find the man that murdered that pore drunken breed. Quit takin' orders from R.T. Barnes and work at yore job like a white man orter!"

Tad's voice was now harsh, brittle. His eyes were reddish-grey slits as he leaped, knocking out the candlelight. His two hands, fastened by the heavy steel handcuffs, struck the sheriff square in the face. In that darkness, in the confusion, Tad fought his way to the door and jerked it open. He had grabbed his gun from the table and now shoved it into the waistband of his trousers. Then he was outside. Big Joe was right behind him. The big cowboy shut the door and fastened the outside bar.

Together they swung aboard the first two horses they found. Jerking the bridles off the other horses, they hazed them into the night.

In the cabin the sheriff and the others were making a desperate effort to break down the heavy plank door. The cabin had no windows. It would take some minutes to break free.

"I'm obliged, Joe," said Tad, when they had set the posse afoot, "for yore help. I knowed I could count on you."

"I got me them Lazy B fellers," said Joe. "Spotted 'em just as the candle went out and I rocked 'em to sleep with my gun barrel. Nice, clean little fight. Directly we git far enough away, I'll saw off them bracelets. Always carry a saw blade or two in your hat band for good luck. Ben taught me that, years ago, when him and me worked together in New Mexico.

"Man, there's a foxy cuss, ol' Ben. Figgers things out. Like he figgered they might track you to the loco trapper's cabin. So he tells me to build to that sheriff an' don't let him outta sight. And I'm to see what I kin do when the play comes right. Dog-gone, but Ben'll have big fits an' little uns when he hears how yuh bawled out that sheriff gent. Then he'll go off to hisself an' chuckle for an hour. He told me you was mule-headed, bull-headed, bone-headed, and as game as a rooster. And he told me if I let you git hurt, he'd bend a gun barrel across my skull. And mister, I'm dog-goned if I don't actually believe he'd do it.

"Ben's a wart hawg, a plumb wart hawg. I'd hate him for an enemy but I'd ask for no better man to have for a friend. And Tad, that li'l ol' sawed-off, hammered-down, bow-legged feller is the best friend you ever made. And I don't bar even yore daddy. I've heard Ben cuss yuh till he was plumb tuckered out. That night ride yuh made. You bawlin' out R.T. and Wayne Wallace. Man, how Ben cussed! Cussed till tears came into his eyes and he told us cowboys that if ary man of us ever quit yuh, he'd take a dull knife an' scalp us, then cut us apart an' feed us to the hawgs. Seems like he was some wild in his younger days, and you kinda remind him o' when he was a bone-headed young fool. If yuh know what I mean, Tad. No harm meant."

"I know what yuh mean, Joe," Tad grinned. "Got that saw blade handy?"

Free of the handcuffs, Tad and Joe rode on into the night.

"Figger on huntin' up John Lockhart, Tad?"

"That was what I had in mind, but it's just runnin' into another trap. The law wants me. The evidence against me is strong. That sheriff ain't losin' no brotherly love on me right now. He's obeyin' R.T.'s orders, and they'll probably plug me on sight if they ketch me. I'll hide out in the badlands till it's safe to show up at the Burnt Ranch.

"You better quit me here and take word to Uncle Ben about Cree Antoine. John Lockhart knows who killed my dad. Uncle Ben has a hunch who did the job. The same man rapped Bob Lockhart on the head. The same man killed Cree Antoine. The same man will kill Ben and me and you and John Lockhart if he gits the chance. I'm gamblin' that the killer is either R.T.

189

or Wayne Wallace. it's the same man that killed Rogers Curtis that's doin' all this ornery work. Uncle Ben and John Lockhart know aplenty. We better split up here, Joe. I'll hang and rattle till — Listen!"

"Some horsebackers comin', Tad!"

They could hear the sound of shod hoofs, the voices of men. They pulled off the trail into the brush.

Through the moonlight that was blotched with the shadows of scrub pines they made out a dozen riders coming down off a ridge.

"Bet a new hat, Joe, that'll be Wayne Wallace and some o' his outfit. If either o' these horses nicker, we'll be in a real tight place."

But even as he spoke, Joe's horse nickered. Tad saw Wayne Wallace and his men rein up short. The next moment Tad and Joe were riding through the treacherous shadows, spurring their horses down a shale bank. Shots ripped through the night as Wayne Wallace and his men sighted the fugitives in the moonlight.

Hard to tell where man or horse was headed for, as Tad and Joe raced for safety. Their horses were sliding down the steep slope. Below was a black pit of darkness.

Joe's sliding horse struck a tree, pawed desperately to keep its feet, then turned over.

Tad, just behind, quit his horse, just in time. From below came the splashing of water as the two horses hit the creek.

"Hurt, Joe?" asked Tad as the bullets snarled around them.

"Me? Nope. What shape you in, Tad?"

"All in one piece. We're set afoot if we don't slide down after them horses. All set?"

"All set."

The bank was almost perpendicular, with a twenty-foot drop into the cold water below where the two horses were floundering around, desperately trying to get out on the far side.

It was dark as the inside of a black hat. And there was a pile-up, there in the water, as the two men tried to grab their horses. The water was about four feet deep — swimming water, almost. Hoofs threshed around. The two men fought with grim, silent desperation to get the horses under control. The black current was carrying them down through a trough between the black shale walls. Bullets sprayed the water, there in the darkness.

Now Tad's horse started downstream, blowing hard, frightened. Tad was clinging to the horse's tail. Close behind him came the other horse, whistling, terrified, pawing the water. Tad called back over his shoulder.

"Yuh all right, Joe?"

"Yeah. I'm — " Joe's voice slipped into silence.

Tad knew that something was wrong. Tad let go his horse's tail and then, just in time, swam to the bank as Joe's horse, a lunging black blot, went past. He caught a glimpse of Joe's threshing arms, in the dark — arms pawing the water.

As the two horses went downstream, Tad made for the struggling Joe. The water was not over four or five feet deep, but the current was swift, treacherous. Tad grabbed Joe as the big cowboy was going under. Joe fought him with that crazy panic of the drowning man. He pulled Tad under — once — again.

Joe's powerful grip was that of a grizzly. Water filled Tad's eyes and nose and mouth. Both he and Joe were fully clothed. They were going under again when Tad, fighting like a madman, got his six-gun free. He struck blindly at the drowning cowpuncher who fought him. Again and again, in this seconds between life and death, he struck at Joe's head. Then he felt Joe's grip relax. Towing Joe's limp form, he struck out downstream.

On either side were the perpendicular shale banks. The current carried them along. Tad spat water, coughed, tightened his grip on Joe's shirt collar. Tad's brain seemed water-logged. That blackness all around! He wondered if he had gone deaf or if those killers had quit shooting. Didn't matter. Death was dragging at him and Joe now, there in the swirling black water. He hoped he hadn't hit Joe too hard.

Thoughts of a hundred and one things flashed through his brain like flickering pictures thrown on a screen, some dim, others vivid. He kept fighting to hold Joe's head above water. Tad had learned to swim in the treacherous waters of the Missouri and Milk Rivers. He couldn't remember when he wasn't able to swim. Water held no fear for him, even now. No more than he had been afraid of a bronc until that day when Mickey Finn, the big roan man-killer, had dragged him, like this black current was dragging him now — perhaps to death.

Fear tightened its ugly grip on his heart — fear of death, fear of being carried down across jagged rocks by the water, taking Joe with him to death; being smashed and broken on the rocks, or else sucked under by the water, smothered, drowned.

For a few minutes, he fought with a terrible, frantic desperation to climb the steep, slippery bank, dragging Joe with him. But the shale gave way under his clutching hand. The strong current carried him and Joe on down between those high, black walls.

Seconds or minutes, they were endless hours to Tad Addison. He fought off his fears and, floating to save his strength, held Joe's head high above the black current and made his whispered prayer to God.

The current became more swift. The water suddenly became shallow. Tad, using his last bit of strength, dragged Joe's big bulk to the grassy bank, at the canyon's mouth.

There were the two horses, standing on the bank, weary, blowing hard. Tad went to work on big Joe, using every trick he knew to revive the man. After what seemed years, Joe's eyes opened. Tad laughed shakily as he watched Joe sit up. Joe coughed and spluttered, then grinned weakly.

"Havin' been raised on the Texas plains," he later told Tad, "I never did learn to swim."

20

COLD, soaked to the skin, just out of the jaws of death, Tad Addison and the cowboy called Joe sat there on the ground, shivering, their teeth chattering.

"I'd give a lot to know where we are," said Tad, as he poured water out of his boots.

"And I'd swap yuh the information, Tad, for a warm fire and some dry clothes and a quart o' red-eye."

"Yuh mean yuh know where we — Looky yonder, pardner. There's yore fire."

As near as Tad could make out they had landed at the mouth of a badland canyon that spread out toward the bottom lands where the creek emptied into the Missouri River. And not more than three hundred yards distant was the light of a camp fire.

"We're in another tight spot, Tad," whispered Joe.

"More posse gents?"

"Not exactly. One of R.T.'s camps. I'll bet a spotted horse they're holdin' a bunch of cattle here. There's water and feed here. One trail in, another that leads out. Somethin' like that hidden coral an' soap hole you located. Us boys had this spotted, but you kin take it from me, we didn't come down the crick like we come tonight, to find the place. There's a corral over yonder. Come daylight, them Lazy B cowboys will be movin' the cattle from that big corral on to safer range. They'll be Lockhart's cattle. Lockhart's boundary line ain't more than a mile away. While the sheriff's men and half the cow country is trailin' you, Wayne Wallace's cow thieves are workin' on Lockhart's cattle."

"Know the trail out, Joe?"

"I think I could find it if I had to."

"And yuh know the trail in from the

Lockhart range?"

"I kin make a stab at locatin' it."

"I'm beginnin' to git the place located, now," said Tad. "This is close to where you boys was shovin' them Lazy B cattle back when yuh got bushwhacked and one o' the bushwackers was either Bob Lockhart or a dead ringer for Bob."

"That's right, Tad. It was right after that fracas when one o' the boys got shot, that I located this place. I told Ben about it. It's a good place to hold a hundred head o' cattle, then drift 'em out on to R.T.'s range where they'll be butchered and sold to the mines where R.T. has a beef contract. I know that as many as five dressed beef is delivered at a time. And only one Lazy B hide to show for the five dead critters. I dunno if R.T. knows it, but I got my suspicions. And I've sighted Wayne Wallace here at this place with his rustlers."

"Still got yore gun, Joe?"

"Still got the old hawg laig, Tad.

And a carbine on my saddle. What you aimin' to do?"

"How do yuh feel?" Tad gave the big cowboy a question instead of an answer.

"Kinda water-logged, cold, my head feels like yuh'd worked me over with an axe. But outside o' that I feel like a three-year-old that's been grain-fed."

"How many men you figger will be over yonder?"

"About three-four. The cattle is in the corral, which is more like a tight wire trap than a corral. It's made o' barb wire. A twelve-mile trap that holds six, eight acres. They don't have to stand night guard. Just sit around the fire an' swap lies. They'll have a jug." There was a sort of eager, wistful note in the big cowboy's voice. He was shivering. His voice came through set teeth that would chatter if his jaw muscles relaxed. He had just escaped drowning, and Tad's gun barrel had made lumps on his head.

"We're in need of a fire and some

dry duds, Joe," said Tad. "A hot whisky would take the chill out of a man's bones. What do yuh say we capture that layout, swap off these wet duds, and spend the rest of the evenin' tellin' them boys stories about Mary had a little lamb and how Bo-Peep lost her sheep? We'll make sheepherders outta them tough lazy B cowhands. No use settin' here shiverin'. Yuh game?"

Joe got to his feet and examined his six-gun. "Ben didn't lie none when he said you was shore hard to handle. I'm with yuh, Tad. We better go afoot. Take our carbines. Give 'em a little surprise party. They might open up on us if we rode up boldlike."

Together they crept up on the group around the camp fire. They saw four men sitting around the blaze, smoking, eating, taking an occasional drink from the big brown jug.

Tad nudged Joe with his elbow. Joe nodded. Then Tad's voice, flat, menacing, called out.

"The first one o' yuh snakes that

tries to rattle, I'll kill him. Lift 'em high to'rds the moon, cowboys, or we'll start shootin'. Stand up there on yore feet and paw high in the air."

The four men, startled, uncertain, obeyed sullenly.

"Now shed yore guns and strip off yore clothes, one at a time. Beginnin' with that purty-lookin' gobbler with the red whiskers, I'm givin' yuh each just one minute to strip to yore hide. All right there, red whiskers. Skin outta yore clothes."

The lanky man with red whiskers snarled something and whirled. Tad and Joe shot almost at the same instant. Their bullets tore through the tall man's hat. And now it was Joe's voice that called out.

"The next time we shoot, red feller, the bullets won't be spoilin' no hat. If I was a bounty hunter, I'd collect me four hides right now. I know yore brands. The red gent is wanted in Idaho for mail robbery. You sawed-off gent with the black hat is wanted in

Colorado for killin' a breed in a fight over too many aces in one deck. You slim gent in the faded mackinaw is wanted in Canada. You big son in the checkered shirt killed a drunken prospector, in Wyoming. I know yuh all. I'd be proud to collect yore bounty money if yuh act up. Do like Tad Addison says. Shed yore guns, then yore clothes. Then step over an' line up. Come on, yuh red-muzzled skunk. Git goin'."

One by one they shed their gun belts and their clothes. now they stood there, bare to the skin, shivering at the edge of the fire. For the night was none too warm, down there in the badlands.

Tad and Joe tied the men up with their own catch ropes, then selected what clothes they needed. Hot whiskies warmed them. Then, after throwing the assortment of guns in the brush, they let the four men put on what clothes were left over.

"I'd hate to be ketched dead in these duds," said Joe, as they tied up their prisoners again, then threw more wood on the fire.

Tad left Joe guarding the prisoners and prowled around the camp. In a few minutes he returned, carrying a bundle of clothes. Fancy boots, Californian pants foxed with buckskin, a tailored shirt with initialled pockets, an expensive Stetson.

"And the horse in the corral is Bob Lockhart's Black Agate," he told Joe as he dropped Bob Lockhart's clothes on the ground. "Here's Bob's hat and white chaps. Here's his clothes. His saddle is there at the corral. But in the same corral is another bald-faced, stockin'-legged horse that belongs to Juanita Barnes. Dead ringer for Black Agate. So it still don't tell us much unless somebody talks. Two o' these men work for R.T., Joe. The other two work for John Lockhart."

"And all four of 'em are wanted by the law," added Joe grimly.

"Let's try red whiskers, Tad. I bet if a man was to tie him up and set fire to that beard he sprouts, he'd give up head like a calf gittin' branded. Let's try 'im out."

Joe jerked the red-whiskered man to his feet and started off into the shadows beyond the fire.

"Ride herd on the others, Tad, while I make medicine with this red-whiskered range tramp."

Joe shoved his prisoner ahead of him. At the fire, Tad eyed the other three whose hands were tied behind their backs as they lay on the ground.

Minutes dragged by. Then came a man's hoarse cry of pain — muffled cursing — a shot. A few moments later the big cowboy called Joe came back to the fire. He ejected an empty shell from his .45 and shoved a fresh cartridge into the empty chamber. Then he helped himself to a drink.

"The red feller wouldn't talk, Tad. I'll try another. There's five hundred on that red-muzzled gent, dead or alive. Well, it ain't every day a man kin pick up five hundred dollars. I'm takin' out the little gent that killed that Colorado breed. I bet he'll talk before I'm done with him. Keep an eye on the other two snakes, Tad. Come on, short feller. I'm takin' my pocket knife and I'm goin' to whittle on yuh some. Yuh'd look purtier without them ears, anyhow. Git along." He kicked the snarling man to his feet and started off with him.

"Don't Joe!" called Tad, his face white. "Don't! Killin' that one man was bad enough!"

"We ain't got all night," said Joe. "Besides, we got to git talk outta these gents. This ain't a tea party. They'll talk or they'll git what the red feller got. Git along, short man."

21

AGAIN Tad waited uneasily, there at the fire. From the darkness beyond came a jumble of sounds — a man's hoarse pleading, muffled talking. Then there was silence. Big Joe came back — alone. He carried an open jack-knife in his hand. There was a grim smile on his tight-lipped mouth as he wiped the blood from the bone-handled stock knife. Then he jerked one of the other two men to his feet and took a red-hot pothook off from the coals where he had put it.

"I'm brandin' this un, Tad."

Tad was on his feet. His face was white, drawn.

"Have yuh gone loco, Joe? This is inhuman! I ain't lettin' yuh, I tell you!"

Big Joe's gun covered Tad. Joe's face was twisted in a snarl.

"I'm doin' this, Anderson! I'm makin' these sons talk or I'll leave their carcasses for the buzzards. Stand where yuh are or I'll have to hurt yuh!"

Tad's hand was creeping toward his gun. Joe's gruff snarl threatened him. Had big Joe gone plumb loco?

It was then, as Tad faced the big cowboy, that he saw the left eye, bloodshot, menacing, wink.

"This is my show, understand that, Addison?" growled big Joe and again he winked. And Tad caught the flicker of a grim smile behind that snarling growl.

"All right, Joe. But it's murder."

"Not when there's a price on their scalps, it ain't murder," was Joe's hard-bitten reply. "Guard that slim feller. He's likely to try to rabbit on yuh. Now I'll git along with this brandin'. I'll run a Lazy B across his withers so's R.T. will know him when he finds his carcass."

The prisoner, white-lipped, on the verge of begging for mercy, was dragged away. Tad eyed the remaining prisoner. He saw a lean unwashed face, pale eyes set too close together on either side of a thin nose, bloodless lips that twitched. He was a man in his late thirties, perhaps; a man with the furtive cunning of a coyote. He stared at Tad as he sat upon the ground, his hands tied behind his back.

Now, from down near the creek, came the groaning of a man in terrible pain; Joe's heavy voice, muffled, growling questions, muffled replies; Joe's cursing — then the abrupt roar of a .45, and then silence.

Sweat beaded the face of the prisoner at the fire. His face twitched spasmodically. He was breathing like a spent runner.

"Don't let that devil take me, Addison. I'll talk! I'll tell yuh all I know! About the whole deal! And I'll tell the truth. Only don't let that big devil torture me, then kill me. I'll talk! I swear I'll tell all of it! About Zack Addison and that Cree Antoine breed. And about how I've heard 'em talk about Rogers Curtis bein' killed. Only yuh'll have to protect me from that big, torturin' devil. He'll kill me if he takes me out there. He'll kill me because he's afraid I'll talk too much — *about him*!"

Tad stared hard into the pale, fear-stricken eyes. What was the man getting at, anyhow? What did he mean?

The wretched, cowering man was talking now in a harsh whisper — begging, groveling, sobbing for his life. He was babbling a partly coherent story of Zack Addison's murder and the murder of Cree Antoine. And Tad listened. He kept wondering what was keeping big Joe. The fear-gripped prisoner was telling Tad that Joe was one of the Lazy B rustlers. Joe was one of the killers hired by Wayne Wallace. Plainly, the poor devil feared big Joe.

"Take me away, Addison. Jail. Anywhere. They want me in Canada for horse stealin'. Take me there. Where I'll be safe. Where Wayne Wallace can't git me. Where R.T. can't locate me and put that big Joe devil on my trail. Let's git away, Addison! He'll kill me if I don't git away. Then he'll kill you! He's Wayne Wallace's killer? He's R.T.'s undercover spy at Burnt Ranch, I tell yuh! and he killed them boys because he was scared they'd tell on him. Addison, let's git away from here!"

The man's terror was convincing. He wasn't lying. Tad edged back into the black shadows. What if big Joe were as treacherous as this sobbing derelict claimed? But Tad could not believe that of big Joe. Impossible! And yet, what did he know of big Joe — or Uncle Ben?

The click of a gun hammer sounded. Tad rolled back into the black shadows, dragging the terrified prisoner with him. A shot ripped out of the darkness. There was another shot, then silence, broken by the rattling cough of a wounded man.

Tad's prisoner tried to yell out, but

Tad clamped his hand across the man's mouth.

"That first shot was meant for you, you yellow coward," whispered Tad in the man's ear. "Somebody took a pot shot at yuh. Then somebody else potted him. Lie quiet, yuh fool."

Then the gruff voice of big Joe came out of the night. "Where are yuh, Tad?"

The prisoner was shaking like a man stricken with a chill. His whispered voice was choked terror.

"Kill 'im, Tad. Don't let 'im git us!"

"Shut up," whispered Tad. Then he called out: "Where are yuh, Joe?"

"In the brush. Don't go near that fire. Keep in the dark. Shoot at anything that moves. There might be some more o' these snakes hid in the brush. Got that prisoner?"

"I got him, Joe."

"Is he hit?"

"No. Who was it that — "

"That tried to kill him when he

was jabberin' like a magpie? One o' his pardners. Hang on to him while I fetch the horses. Ask that yaller coyote how many more is hid around here?"

"How many?" growled Tad.

"No more, Tad. That must 'a' been the guard from the upper trail. He must 'a' heard big Joe shoot that red-whiskered feller. He snuck up. Heard me talk. Or else he shot at you. I tell yuh, Tad, Joe's the big ramrod. He's aimin' to kill us both."

"Shut up," growled Tad. If Joe was in cahoots with Wayne Wallace, then Joe would get his when he made a gun play. But it was hard to believe that big Joe was a killer — even with the evidence against him.

Joe rode on Bob Lockhart's Black Agate. He was leading Midnight and another saddled horse.

"Time we hauled freight outta here, Tad. Load that coyote on to that bay horse. I saddled the Midnight horse for yuh."

Tad lifted the cowering renegade into the saddle.

"Untie his hands, Tad," said Joe. "I got a hunch we're goin' for a fast ride. Listen, you coyote, when Tad give you them bridle reins, you do what I tell yuh. Try to rabbit on us and I'll kill yuh, like I killed them other things. Now lead the way outta here an' no tricks."

22

BIG Joe rode behind the rustler, leaving Tad to follow behind. Tad reckoned that Joe had heard the babbling of the renegade. Joe was giving Tad the chance to shoot him if he believed the squealing coward.

They went up the winding trail and across a timbered ridge. Nobody spoke. For an hour, perhaps, they kept on. Then Joe called a halt. He called Tad to one side.

"Take this coyote to the Burnt Ranch. If Ben ain't there, wait for him. I knowed this rat would squeal when he had the fear in him."

"Yuh heard what he said about you, Joe?"

"Shore thing. And let him keep on talkin' his head off. Git it down in writin'. The whole thing. About me bein' Wayne Wallace's killer an' all of it."

"Joe," said Tad, facing the big cowpuncher, "you killed them three men in cold blood. We better have a show-down right now."

"Keep yore shirt tail tucked in, Tad. I didn't kill nobody. Not even the last un that slipped up on yuh. I just gagged them others an' hog-tied 'em, then shot off my gun an' made it sound like a killin'. I did stick that one feller with my jackknife so's to git blood on it. I was playin' the slim gent for a squealer. And from the way he turned loose with the chin music, I figger I sized him up right.

"Now hang on to that chatterin' magpie. He's our big bet. Don't let him git shot. I'm bettin' that Wayne Wallace is due to show up before long, there at that corral. I'm meetin' him there, and I'm leadin' him off on the wrong trail while you take this coyote to the Burnt Ranch. Turn him over to Ben."

"Yo're meeting Wayne Wallace?"

Big Joe grinned and rolled a smoke.

"Didn't yuh hear that coyote tell yuh how I was Wayne Wallace's undercover spy?" he asked.

"Listen, Joe, come clean with a man. What's it all about?"

"Yuh'll learn it all before long, Tad. You just haze that coyote on to the Burnt Ranch an' make him talk. Tell Ben that I'm leadin' Wayne Wallace an' his men off the trail for a spell. Tell him how yuh called the sheriff. And tell him that when this is over and done with, I'm goin' to bed with a jug an' sleep warm for a month. and I ain't takin' no bath. I'm so full o' water now that every time I move, it gurgles inside o' me."

"Joe, I don't care what that squealin' rat says about yuh. I don't care what you say about yoreself bein' Wayne Wallace's undercover spy. You've acted like a man and a smart man at that. Yuh keep makin' me feel like I'm just a kid. Shake hands, Joe?"

"Proud o' the honor, yuh young mule-headed wart hawg. And thanks for thinkin' I'm a man."

They shook hands, then Joe rode away, back along the trail they had come. Tad got his prisoner and headed for the ranch.

The stars hung low in the moonlit sky. Between Tad's legs was the horse he had broken for Juanita. He thought of her now as he headed for the Burnt Ranch. He wondered where she was, what she was doing, what she was thinking.

It seemed to Tad like Life or Fate, or whatever you might call it, had picked him up and thrown him headlong into a whirlpool filled with snags. What was it all about? What part was he playing in this fast-moving drama that centered around the Burnt Ranch? R.T. Barnes — what was R.T.'s part in it? John Lockhart's friendship — was it sincere? Bob Lockhart — how deeply was Bob Lockhart involved in this rustling game that Wayne Wallace was playing? And who was Uncle Ben, anyhow, and what was that little old cowpuncher's game?

And big Joe, who was a human puzzle! And how much of it all did Juanita understand?

He dozed in his saddle as he and his prisoner rode on. Tad rubbed tobacco in his eyes to keep them open.

Dawn was creeping over the broken skyline when they rode into the Burnt Ranch.

Uncle Ben was at the barn. The little old cowpuncher stared at Tad as if he were seeing a ghost. Then he began swearing huskily, his puckered blue eyes like sapphire lights, there in the lantern light of the big log barn.

"They fetched word that you was dead, Tad. That you an' Joe was drowned."

"They had it wrong, Uncle Ben."

"So I see."

Uncle Ben swore like a mule skinner for five minutes before Tad could cut him off. The cowpunchers around the barn, every man of them heavily armed, grinned. Tad's pasty-faced, pale-eyed prisoner smiled in sickly fashion.

"I got a feller here," Tad finally managed to say, "that has some talkin' to do. Let's go to the house."

"Talkin' to do? Where's Joe?"

"Joe went back. I'll tell yuh about it later. Any news about Bob Lockhart?"

"Bob's got an even chance to life, last report I got from town. Tad, before we talk to this feller, I want to see yuh alone. Things is comin' to a head an' comin' so fast that it makes an old feller's head go round like a buzz saw."

★ ★ ★

In the old-fashioned front room of the log house, Uncle Ben and Tad sat down, facing one another across the littered table. Uncle Ben poured out two drinks, then pawed through some papers. He found the papers he wanted, then leaned back in his old rawhide-seated chair.

"Tad," said little old Uncle Ben, puffing at his pipe, "it's time me an' you had a medicine talk. Providin' anybody kin talk sense into that bronc-fighter's head o' yourn. Of all the hard-mouthed, jug-headed, loco young cowpunchers I ever run acrost — an' I've met aplenty between Mexico an' Canada — you take the first money. John Lockhart tellin' me how you was level-headed! If there's a brain in that bone skull o' yourn that ain't wild, then I'm a Chinaman. John gives me orders how to handle yuh with a hackamore, not a spade bit.

"And what do yuh do? What didn't yuh do? Yuh did everything wrong. Everything. Into the fire outta the fryin' pan. Yuh rode sharpshod where no angel would step. Instead o' usin' yore head, yuh used yore fists an' a six-gun. Never once did yuh do what John Lockhart an 'me wanted you to do. And yuh done more in a few days an' nights than me an' John has been able to do in years. Tad, yuh — Tad, I'd give all I ever had to be what you are right now. Here's howdy, bronc rider!" Old Uncle Ben's voice broke a little as he reached for his glass.

The mistiness of those puckered blue eyes told the story — the story of a man grown past his prime, a man who sees his yesterdays reflected in youth.

When they had put down their empty glasses, Uncle Ben loaded up his old pipe and lighted it.

"We got R.T. on the run, Tad. That sheriff he bought into office has turned in his badge. The man that has taken his place is the man that should 'a' been in long ago. R.T. is at his ranch. He's hid out there, guarded by the men he's hired to guard him. He ain't sleepin' much but he shore is puttin' away the liquor. He sees it a-comin', Tad. He knows that he's goin' to be licked, I reckon. Juanita is with him. She's the only one that's stayin' with him without bein' paid to do so. Tad, you've about smashed R.T., I reckon."

"Me?"

"You. And it was a quick job. R.T.

started to smash you. He didn't give yuh credit for what yuh are. That sheriff has wrote out a full confession which he left before he pulled out for wherever it is that men like him go when they take a gun an' blow their brains out. He didn't lay no blame on you, son. He laid it on R.T. an' laid 'er on thick. Yep, he said aplenty in that confession. I reckon this prisoner you fetched in will tell plenty more. An' that ain't sayin' what Joe will have to tell when he gits here to the Burnt Ranch.

"Tad, R.T. has always wanted this ranch. He had Rogers Curtis murdered. He's been stealin' cattle for years from John Lockhart. He tried to blackmail Bob Lockhart into marryin' Juanita. He didn't know that John Lockhart was wise to the whole thing. Bob Lockhart would marry Juanita in a minute if she'd have him. But she won't have him. She told him so. She told R.T. the same thing, before she climbed out her hotel window to go to the carnival with you. She'd told him, earlier in the evenin'. And she'd told Bob Lockhart the same thing. Called 'em a pair o' crooks and what not, and said that she was going to marry the one man she loved and that man was Tad."

"That's why Bob picked the fight with me?"

"Partly, I reckon. He didn't want to lose his girl. And then R.T. promised Bob he'd hand over them IOU's if he'd beat you up. Bob didn't know what would happen to yuh after he'd knocked yuh cold. Only that you won that fight, it would be you, not Bob Lockhart, that would be in bed with a busted skull. You see, R.T.'s hired skull-buster got drunked up. His orders is to sap the loser o' the fight on the head when he's bein' carried outta the dark alley.

"Not knowin' either you ner Bob, this gent with the blackjack slips up as they're carryin' Bob down the alley to the back door. He raps Bob over the head, then runs for it. But the bartender at the Deuce High, after this blackfeller gits tight, smells a rat. And he slips the blackjack man a few drops that put him to sleep. He wakes up sick an' broke. He talks some. And he talks more when he's put in jail under guard. If Bob Lockhart dies, he'll mebbyso hang. No need for you to be on the dodge now."

"They got me accused of killin' Cree Antoine," said Tad.

"Not no more. I done corralled the feller that murdered Cree Antoine. He's in the hospital with a couple o' busted arms. Wayne Wallace had told the sheriff who killed Antoine, an' so when I read the sheriff's confession, I gathered in Mr. Bushwhacker. He's done some gun clawin', but I winged him. He'll hang, I reckon. He's wanted in Texas for murder."

"You seem to know everything that goes on," said Tad.

"Yep. That's my business, son. Sometimes I'm on to such things even before they happen. Yuh say

Joe's leadin' Wayne Wallace off on a wrong trail? That'll mean he's takin' 'em to that corral an' greased shute at the soap hole. That means I better git saddled up an' goin', Tad. That prisoner will wait. He'll talk tomorrow. You lay down an' take a sleep."

"Sleep? I don't need no sleep. Ben, I got a question to ask and I got to git the right answer."

"Shoot, Tad."

"Who killed my father?"

"Wayne Wallace killed him. I don't reckon he meant to, but he did. Wayne was drunk. Yore dad said somethin', an' Wayne hit him. Knocked him cold, an' as he fell, he rolled under the heels o' that big roan bronc. There was another feller with Wayne. The same gent that killed Antoine. Antoine tried to git in the stall to drag Zack out, but Wayne Wallace hit him an' kicked him up the ladder into the loft."

Tad was on his feet now, white-lipped, every nerve pulled taut. He forgot that he was hungry and sleepy and utterly weary in every bone and muscle. He picked up his hat — the hat he had taken from one of the captured rustlers.

"Where yuh headed for, Tad? Where yuh goin'?"

"I'm goin' after Wayne Wallace. I aim to kill him where I find him."

23

TAD threw his saddle on Big Enough. His eyes were like hard, glittering grey lights. Uncle Ben had to hurry to catch up with him. There were half a dozen cowboys behind him.

"Take 'er easy, Tad," advised Uncle Ben, riding alongside him.

Tad was riding his pet horse to the limit. He made no reply for some minutes.

"One thing I own in this world," he said flatly, "is this Big Enough horse. I'll ride him like I owned him. I'll find out, before I'm done, why they sold me the Burnt Ranch."

"I kin tell yuh that as we ride, son. John Lockhart wanted a real man to own the place. He was willin' to pay the difference to have a man of nerve here, a man that R.T. couldn't scare off ner buy off. That's why you got the place dirt cheap. And yuh shore have earned the difference in the price."

"Why didn't John Lockhart buy it?"

"Because he was scared to trust Bob. R.T. had a holt on Bob Lockhart. Bob had a weakness fer whisky and a deck o' cards. R.T. had taken advantage of it. Once Bob married Juanita, old John Lockhart's life wouldn't be worth a Mexican centavo. John Lockhart is yore friend, Tad. He never meant for you to know he'd kinda handed you the Burnt Ranch on a platter. He's always liked you. He always wanted Bob to kinda pattern his ways after yore ways.

"John Lockhart is a square man, Tad. It must 'a' hurt him aplenty to tell Juanita that Bob was no good and that R.T. was usin' her an' Bob. Yep, that's what Senator John Lockhart done. Then he told Juanita that she was goin' to marry the man she loved. That's the kind of a friend he's been to you, Tad Addison. Think 'er over some before yuh say anything about John Lockhart an' the Burnt Ranch deal. John knowed yuh'd make good. But son, he wouldn't want yuh to go chargin' off this a way, killin' Wayne Wallace. There's men hired to hang the hide o' that killin' wolf on the fence."

"Meanin' who, Uncle Ben?"

"Meanin' me an' Joe." Uncle Ben reached into his chaps pocket and pulled out a gold badge. He pinned it on his faded flannel shirt.

"United States marshal!" gasped Tad.

"Yep. Joe's my deputy. Been workin' on this case since before Rogers Curtis got killed. I'm the loco prospector that lived down yonder in the badlands. Just a few months ago I fetched Joe into the game. And the game that Joe plays is dangerous enough for any man. He's helped Wayne Wallace run off horses an' rustle cattle. He's supposed to be Wayne Wallace's top hand. And if Wallace finds out who Joe is, it'll be too bad fer Joe."

Uncle Ben was giving Tad plenty to think about as they rode into the red sunrise.

"Better turn back, Tad."

"Wayne Wallace killed my dad," was Tad Addison's brief reply. He urged his Big Enough horse to a long trot.

Mile after mile, they went, down through the badlands. They heard the distant sound of shots. Uncle Ben, riding a gaunt-flanked, leggy dun horse, jerked the carbine from his saddle scabbard.

"If they got Joe," he muttered, letting the big dun horse out to a long lope, "I'll make 'em pay aplenty."

The old fellow's leathery face was grey now. He swung ahead of Tad along the narrow trail. Tad was forced to follow behind. There was something about that little old cowpuncher ahead that tightened Tad's throat — that battered old hat, the white hair beneath, the hunched shoulders, the wiry, sinewy frame of little old Uncle Ben. Uncle Ben, who was a U.S. marshal, a man hunter, was like a little old grey wolf with worn fangs, scarred by many battles.

Down the slope they went, never checking their speed. Ben's big dun was as sure-footed as a goat. Big Enough was following right behind. One of the men behind picked up a bad fall and was swearing roundly. There was no time to look back now. Eyes were ahead, watching the trail, watching below where the enemy waited at that greased chute that dropped at a slant into the deadly soap hole.

They reached the foot of the twisted, steep trail with a rush. Bullets snarled around them. Tad saw Uncle Ben quit his horse while the big dun was hitting a run. Tad followed suit, leaving Big Enough with a leap that piled him up in the brush. He could have sworn that Uncle Ben was shooting, there in mid-air, as he quit his horse.

"Git 'em boys!" shouted Uncle Ben. "Have at 'em!"

Tad saw, in the fraction of a second,

something that chilled his blood. He saw big Wayne Wallace, there at the chute — saw him take an iron-pointed prod and jab at a man who stood in the chute; saw that man lurch forward, slide crazily, drop into that black bog. Then Uncle Ben's gun roared, and Wayne Wallace toppled backward on to the ground, shooting wildly.

Tad quit the brush. A second later he was in the saddle. He felt something like a hot iron stab his shoulder as he jerked his lariat free. As he spurred Big Enough toward the soap hole, he flipped a loop into shape.

He could see a man sinking out there, up to his waist in the black mud that would, in a few moments, suck him under.

Things were happening all around Tad. But he saw only one thing — big Joe going down to that black, horrible death. Tad made a hard throw. The grass rope shot out almost to its last foot. The loop dropped down across Joe's shoulders. Tad took his dallies and whirled Big Enough, the best rope horse in the country. Game-hearted, wise, the horse jerked tight the rope. Shod hoofs bit deeply into the sod. It was a terrific pull — a two-hundred-pound man half-buried in that black, bubbling suction of death. For a moment that seemed an hour, Big Enough dug in, snorting, using every ounce of weight, every bit of skill in his game body — with Tad's voice, panting, sobbing in his furry ears.

"Hang, pony! Hang, old man! Dig in, Big Enough! Dig in, son! Good horse!"

Oblivious of the fight that was going on, Tad and his pet horse dragged big Joe out of the soap hole. Joe, smeared from hair to boots with that black mud, lay like a dead man on solid ground. Tad let go his dallies.

"Good pony," he said.

Tad ran to where Joe lay and with his hands, wiped the mud from Joe's face. Then he found his knife and cut the rope that bound Joe's hands. There was blood oozing through the mud that smeared the big cowboy's shirt. Joe got to his feet dizzily. Through the black smear of mud he grinned at Tad.

"That was good work, Tad. First yuh keep me from drownin', then from this. I'm more than six bits in debt to yuh, pardner."

Now Uncle Ben's staccato profanity brought Tad back to reality. He saw Wayne Wallace, handcuffed to a tree, cursing the pain of a wounded leg and arm. He saw Wayne Wallace's men lined up, hands in the air. And Uncle Ben, his old cedar-handled .45 dangling in his hand, was coming toward them at a bow-legged trot. Then things went black, and Tad's knees buckled under him.

Dimly, as in a dream, he heard Uncle Ben's voice. Uncle Ben was calling for water and bandages and telling somebody that if Tad Addison died, he'd shove Wayne Wallace into that mud hole.

24

TAD awoke to white sheets, pulled-down blinds, the clean odor of disinfectant, hushed, subdued voices. He looked at the white ceiling. Then he closed his eyes again. He was tired, awfully tired, tired as a played-out horse. It was good to shut his eyes and feel the cool, white sheets around him. Wasn't often that cowboys ever got the feel of white sheets. It was only in hotels or — hospitals. Hospitals — Mickey Finn.

"I'll ride 'im! Let me outta this bed an' I'll ride 'im!"

Strong hands, strong with the strength that goes with gentleness, put Tad back between the cool white sheets.

"Give him to me!" growled Tad. "Gimme that Mickey Finn bronc and I'll ride 'im."

"Shore thing yuh'll ride 'im, Tad.

But not today." Uncle Ben's leathery face showed above the bed, then Senator John Lockhart's face, and the comely features of a nurse, with hair the color of gold. A stranger was with them.

Tad shut his eyes again, just for a second. Then he opened them. He was remembering things now, in a dazed way.

"He's all right," said Uncle Ben. "Tougher'n rawhide. How yuh feelin', son?"

Tad grinned faintly.

"Howdy, Ben. Would yuh fetch me a barrel o' cold water?"

"Ten barrels, if yuh say so. But the nurse will feed yuh the water. I ain't sterilized or somethin'. John, I told yuh he'd come out a-rearin'. Now Tad, you lay on the bed ground. Take 'er easy."

"What ails me?"

"Bullet hole in yore carcass, that's all. It's out, now. Yo're in the hospital with Bob Lockhart an' big Joe, an' both of 'em is waitin' for yuh to git well enough to play a game o' cooncan er rummy."

"Bob Lockhart's here?"

"Right over here in the next stall, Tad."

Tad twisted his head. Bob Lockhart, his head bandaged, grinned and waved a salute.

"The cots are too far away, Tad, or I'd shake with yuh. That's providing you'd shake hands with a man that — "

"I'll shake with yuh, Bob, any time."

"The tomahawk's buried, Tad?" Bob Lockhart's voice held a queer note of pleading.

"Buried so deep she'll never be dug up, Bob."

Then Tad saw Senator John Lockhart standing there. The old cowman walked between the two beds. He took Tad Addison's hand in one of his, Bob's hand in his other hand.

"I wouldn't swap this moment for all the white-faced cattle in Montana," he said, his voice husky with emotion. "Now get well, both of you wild Injuns."

A few moments later Tad was saying howdy to big Joe, in the cot the other side of him.

"Took 'em twelve hours, Tad, to wash off that mud. An' I swore I'd never take another bath in water."

So began Tad's days in the hospital, days between white sheets. And one night, after the lights were out, he listened while Bob Lockhart told of his entanglement with R.T. and Wayne Wallace. How they had blackmailed him into lending Wayne his Black Agate horse and his rodeo chaps and hat. How they had used him until he had, in a moment of desperation, told them that he was finished with them. And how R.T. had threatened him with a penitentiary sentence. But everything was all right now. Bob was going back to the ranch. He was through with that wild life that had so nearly trapped him with death.

Tad let Bob talk on. Then he cursed Bob out for keeping him and Joe awake with a lot of talk that nobody wanted to hear, anyhow. And then they all three got called down by the night nurse because Joe played his harmonica while Tad and Bob tried to get some kind of cowboy harmony out of the 'Cowboy's Lament'.

It was Uncle Ben who brought news to Tad about Juanita Barnes and R.T. John Lockhart had refused to prosecute R.T. Juanita and her father had gone to California. R.T. was a sick man, broken in health. Juanita was his one and only friend, Juanita had changed, so Uncle Ben hinted. She was staying with her father out of loyalty, not because of any love for him. But Tad remembered what she had told him that night of the carnival — how she would always hate him if he should ever hurt her father.

Then, one day, weeks later, at the Burnt Ranch where Tad was regaining his strength, John Lockhart had a talk with Tad — a talk that never was repeated beyond the room where Senator John Lockhart and Tad Addison sat.

"R.T. might have gone far, except for his greediness, Tad. His wife, the mother of Juanita, was a wonderful woman, a saint. I am telling you what no man on earth knows, or ever shall know. I loved her. She loved me. I had lost my wife. Her husband was little better than a ruthless brute. And yet that love never went beyond a handclasp and the promise I made her, just before she died, that I would safeguard the happiness of her little daughter Juanita. Juanita loves you, Tad. She will come back one day, or you will go to her. Then that promise I made the woman I loved, will be fulfilled. Let nothing on this earth keep you and Juanita from your happiness."

Tad listened in silence. He wanted to hope for that happiness. But inside his heart was a leaden lump. In his memory were Juanita's words. "Perhaps, inside my heart, I love you. But I could turn that love into hate if you ever harmed my father."

25

IT was good to be back in the saddle again, good to smell the smoke of a branding fire, to hear the bawling of cattle, to taste the round-up grub and listen to the 'hoorawing' of the cowboys as they sat around of an evening swapping yarns.

But for Tad Addison it was even better than that. He was running his own round-up wagon, leading circles of a frosty morning, cutting his own steers into the day herd, handling men who took his orders.

Senator John Lockhart, before he left for California for the winter, had convinced Tad that the young cowpuncher had earned the Burnt Ranch.

"You cleaned up that Wayne Wallace gang, Tad. They hung Wallace and two o' his worst killers. The others will stay in the pen a long time. But that's not all. You made a real man outta Bob. That's what counts. The Burnt Ranch is yours. Forget about it. I'm as proud of you as if you were my own son. I wish Zack were alive to see you now. I'm off for Santa Barbara tonight. I'll see you in the spring. Good luck, Tad."

Santa Barbara, out there in California, was where R.T. and Juanita had gone. Tad had wanted to ask about R.T., but John Lockhart hated questions. So Tad had kept still. But he knew that the bank had taken over R.T.'s outfit and that Uncle Ben had put in a crew of men with big Joe as boss.

Long days in the saddle, hard work — it was good medicine for Tad who had things to forget.

Sometimes on guard at night, riding around the bedded beef herd, when the moon shone like a cold white ball, he thought of all that had happened. Mostly his thoughts were of Juanita, out there in California with R.T., whose health was broken. She'd be hating Tad now.

Uncle Ben had turned in his badge and was handling the beef herd for Tad. And no better beef man ever cursed out a cowboy for trotting tallow off a fat native steer.

Tad and Ben went to Chicago with the last shipment of beef. They took in all the shows and good restaurants, then came back to settle down for the winter. There was work to do and plenty of it. Winter was crowding close. Tad sent the men to the several line camps for the winter's job of 'rawhiding'.

Now and then he saw Bob Lockhart, and they would often work together gathering cattle that would need feeding. They had become the best of friends now.

Bob and Tad were in town ordering winter supplies when the news of R.T.'s death reached Black Coulee. John Lockhart sent a long wire to Bob saying that R.T. had died of heart disease and that they — John Lockhart and Juanita — were bringing him back for burial. Bob made the funeral arrangements.

On a raw November day the hearse, drawn by a pair of black horses that had been raised by Zack Addison, met the train. All of Black Coulee attended the funeral.

Tad had seen Juanita at the hotel. She was dressed in black and looked pale and tired. They were face to face, there in the lobby. Juanita passed Tad as if he were a stranger. Tad saddled his horse and started for the ranch. There was a blizzard coming, and it hit him about dark. He was half-frozen when he reached the Burnt Ranch, and Uncle Ben worked for hours with a tub of snow and hot toddies to bring Tad out of it.

The long winter nights found Tad playing endless games of chess with Uncle Ben.

Sometimes Ben Lockhart would come over for a few days, or Tad would ride over with Ben to the Lockhart ranch. now and then big Joe came over.

Tad knew that John Lockhart had taken Juanita back to Santa Barbara. He had read it in the Black Coulee *Journal*.

His days were spent in the saddle, bucking snowdrifts and visiting the line camps; in reading everything he could find, playing chess, waiting for the spring chinooks and green grass and the calf round-up that would break the white monotony of winter.

Spring found Tad grown heavier, stronger. His frost-blackened face showed faint lines around his eyes and the corners of his mouth. He looked older.

Before the calf work began, on the pool horse round-up where the Lazy B, the Circle, and Tad's outfit worked together, Tad got a surprise. The first day's gathering of horses, over on the Lazy B range, held a big roan gelding.

"There's your Mickey Finn outlaw, Tad," said Bob Lockhart. "In good shape, too. Goin' to top him off for us?"

Tad forced a faint grin. Inside, he had grown suddenly cold. Through his brain flashed the memory of being dragged by that wicked roan outlaw.

"I'm savin' him for the Fourth o' July show," he replied. And that night he slept but little. In his dreams he was being dragged to death. Again and again he suffered the same nightmare. Under his tarp and blankets he was wet with cold perspiration. And he told himself, over and over, that he would keep that promise to ride Mickey Finn at the Fourth of July contest.

The Fourth of July was the big day of the year on the calendar of the little cow town of Black Coulee, Montana. The calf round-up was over, and the cowboys from all the outfits in that part of the country were in town, pockets filled with crumpled bills, their spurs let out to the town notch. Every sort of rig was there, from dead-X wagons filled with Indians from the reservation, to top buggies with silver-painted wheels. Women from the ranches were dressed in their best clothes that gave off the combined odor of mothballs and the cologne sold at the Mercantile. Youngsters from the ranches were filling up on candy and water melon and ice cream. Tomorrow there would be a run on the Mercantile for castor oil.

Grey-bearded cowmen, dressed in their town clothes, were standing around swapping talk that had been bottled up all the long winter. Now and then they would move inside the nearest saloon.

Tin-horn gamblers were running any kind of a game a cowboy could ask for.

Blanketed Indians were staring into store windows — squaws with round-eyed, fat-cheeked papooses of all ages. Some of them were hanging around the depot waiting to sell polished buffalo horns and buckskin moccasins decorated with beadwork and colored porcupine quills.

Cowboys were everywhere — walking

up and down the broad plank sidewalks or riding down the street toward the fairgrounds, some leading broncs or running horses, some in overalls, others dressed in gayer raiment. It was a good-natured crowd, talking, laughing, with the popping of firecrackers and six-guns, and now and then a fight — all under a blue sky and a warm sun.

The morning was devoted to horse-racing; the wild pursuit of a greased pig; potato races, foot races for men, women, boys, and fat men; the roping contests and the bulldogging.

Bob Lockhart won first money in the calf roping and steer tying. Big Joe won the bulldogging.

At noontime the town was packed with visitors from the range. The crowd ate hamburger sandwiches and kept their seats in the grandstand because the bronc riding, the big event of the day, was to begin at one o'clock.

In the corral with the broncs was the big, grain-fed roan outlaw, Mickey Finn. One of the Burnt Ranch cowboys had brought him in.

"Where's Tad Addison?" asked the arena director. "Ain't he comin' to town?" The bronc riders were gathered around, drawing their horses.

"I'll draw for Tad," said Bob Lockhart. "Mickey Finn's name ain't in the hat. But I'm drawin' Mickey Finn for Tad Addison. He'll be here to ride when the time comes."

"So far as I'm concerned," said big Joe, also entered in the bronc riding, "Tad's plumb welcome to that roan mankiller. I wouldn't ride that horse for all the cattle in Montana."

Bob Lockhart drew Bad Medicine. Joe got a crop-eared, sunburnt sorrel called Wart Hog.

Uncle Ben rode up. He was to be one of the judges. The little old cowpuncher looked worried.

"Where's Tad?" he asked.

"Nobody's seen him, Ben," said Bob Lockhart. "He said he'd be here. I talked to him yesterday at the Burnt Ranch."

Uncle Ben nodded. "He pulled out for town right after supper. Said he'd like to go alone. Us boys left right after he did. But he ain't showed up in town. Nobody's sighted him all mornin'. His Big Enough horse ain't in the barn."

"What do yuh make of it, Ben?" asked Joe.

"Nothin'. Nothin', only fer two bits I'd take a gun an' kill that Mickey Finn bronc, that's all." And with that cryptic remark he quit his horse and climbed into the judge's stand.

"What did he mean by that, Joe?"

"Search me, Bob. The old man's funny about never spillin' what's on his mind."

They didn't know that Uncle Ben had caught Tad Addison, more than once, there at the Burnt Ranch, squatted in the darkness near Mickey Finn's stall, muttering, sometimes sobbing brokenly. Tad hadn't seen Uncle Ben those nights when he crept from the house to go to the barn where the grain-fed roan outlaw was kept.

TAD was in town. He had ridden in on another horse, leaving Big Enough at a ranch pasture where he had changed horses.

All morning Tad had stayed in the house where he had been born, stayed behind closed blinds. He was alone there with the turbulent memories that filled his brain. He had ridden all night alone, fighting that terrible fear that tore at his heart.

He looked at his watch. It was past noon, nearing the hour when he would have to ride that roan outlaw. It was like waiting to be hanged. There was a bottle of whisky on the dresser. Zack had left it there. Tad uncorked the bottle. Then he saw that picture of himself riding Bad Medicine, a duplicate of the one that hung on the wall at the Deuce High. He corked the dusty bottle without touching the contents. Then he went to the barn and saddled the horse he had ridden to town.

The streets were deserted. Even the Deuce High was closed. Everybody in town was at the fair grounds. Tad headed for the grounds at a lope.

He passed through the gates where the contestants entered. He grinned as best he could as the grizzled, old gateman, swamper from the Deuce High and one of Zack's old cronies, greeted him with a rheumy-eyed, whisky-voiced, "Good luck to ye, Taddy."

Tad gave the old drunkard a handful of bills. Then he rode down in back of the chutes, like a man riding through a dream. He could hear the band playing. He could hear the babble of voices, the voice of the announcer.

"Laydees and gents, I have to announce that the big roan outlaw, Mickey Finn, will have to be turned loose without bein' rode. Tad Addison is — "

"Tad Addison is here!" yelled a cowboy. "Tad's just rode up. Tad's here! Git the chute handlers to saddle that bronc!"

And as the announcer called out that Tad Addison would be coming out of Chute No. 1 a mighty roar of applause filled the grandstand. Then the band struck up, and everybody watched that chute where the big roan was kicking at the planks that caged him.

Uncle Ben quit the judge's stand, handing his stopwatch to somebody. He was down the steep stairway from the elevated stand and hanging on to Tad's arm now.

"Tad, don't ride that big roan. Let 'em turn him out! Don't ride that man-killer, son!"

Tad shook his head, like a man with cobwebs in his brain. Then he grinned at Uncle Ben and Bob Lockhart who rode up.

"Pick me up, Bob?"

"I'll tell a man. Tad, I'll be on hand when yuh go out of the chute. And if

254

Black Agate can't pick up that big roan, then no horse can. Where in Sam Hill have you been hiding? Look up yonder in the stand — there in the main box. Dad's there with Juanita."

But Tad didn't seem to hear. He nodded absently. "Screw that hull down tight on Mickey Finn, Bob."

"But, listen, Tad, Juanita said to — "

"And pull the buckin' strap plenty tight," finished Tad, heading right for the chute that held the roan man-killer.

Everything was blurred, just like in the nightmares that had torn through his sleep so many nights. Tad looked at his taped spurs, then buckled on a pair of wing chaps somebody had handed him. And it was Tad who reached through the planks and jerked tight the bucking strap on Mickey Finn. Then he settled himself into the saddle as the big roan outlaw lunged and tried to fall over backward.

"Give 'im to me!" he growled.

The chute gate swung open. Tad's

spurs raked the roan shoulders as the bawling, squealing outlaw left the chute. He held the halter rope in a loose grip. He fanned the bowed neck with his hat. Underneath him, between his legs, was the worst outlaw horse in the country, limber-legged, sunfishing, twisting, end-swapping Mickey Finn. But Tad Addison was riding, riding as he had never ridden before. He was riding Mickey Finn, the bronc that had put the fear in him. And he was riding Fear right now. He was riding Fear — without grabbing saddle leather, without losing a stirrup; riding straight up, high, wide and handsome.

Tad didn't know that he was yelling as he rode. He didn't remember afterward about the crack of the gun that gave him a qualified ride and the world's championship. He didn't remember cursing and yelling at Bob Lockhart when Bob tried to pick him up. All Tad knew just then was that he was breaking a bronc.

And it was all of ten minutes

later when Tad Addison rode Mickey Finn into the corral — rode him in and unsaddled the big roan. Tad had pushed away the helpers. He had grinned at Bob Lockhart out of a face that was dust-powdered, sweat-streaked.

"I rode 'im, Bob. I'll unsaddle 'im. He's mine. He belongs to me. And some day I'll make outta this big bronc, the best horse a man ever sat on. I done broke Mickey Finn. He's never buckin' again."

Tad was breathing hard. It had been as tough a ride as ever a bronc stomper made. But he was grinning. That fear was gone out of his heart. He had ridden Mickey Finn. He had ridden Fear.

Uncle Ben motioned Bob Lockhart away with a queer smile and a wink.

"Go tell yore dad, Bob," he whispered huskily, "that Tad Addison is a bronc rider. John Lockhart will savvy what I mean."

Tad unsaddled the big roan gelding.

He spent the best part of the next hour caring for the horse and rubbing the big head of the roan man-killer. And it was there in the corral that Juanita Barnes and Bob Lockhart found Tad Addison.

Tad, sweaty, unshaven, grinned at them.

"Got me a Circle horse, Bob, that'll be a shore enough road runner. When yore Circle cowboys foller me on this horse, they better fetch along their lantern an' some grub because I'll be leadin' where they'll have to change three horses to foller me. If yuh don't believe that, ask Mickey. Am I lyin', roan feller?"

"When you get through telling your life's story to that horse," said Bob Lockart, "come on over here and meet a friend of yours. And you're holding up the parade back to town. Tad, there are two horses out here waiting. Two black horses with bald faces and stocking legs. One of those horses is Juanita's Midnight. The other horse, full brother to Midnight is Black Agate. He's yours. You own Black Agate, Tad. I'm giving him to you for keeps, saddle and all. Just like I'm giving you the greatest little girl in the world.

"My dad, John Lockhart, is expecting you at the house after the parade. There'll be a minister there. And if you don't ask me to be best man at the biggest wedding Black Coulee ever saw, I'll lick the tar out of you. And now, Juanita, I'm turning you over to Tad Addison, my best friend. Take care of her, *bronc rider*!"

Other titles in the Linford Western Library:

TOP HAND
Wade Everett

The Broken T was big. But no ranch is big enough to let a man hide from himself.

GUN WOLVES OF LOBO BASIN
Lee Floren

The Feud was a blood debt. When Smoke Talbot found the outlaws who gunned down his folks he aimed to nail their hide to the barn door.

SHOTGUN SHARKEY
Marshall Grover

The westbound coach carrying the indomitable Larry and Stretch headed for a shooting showdown.

FIGHTING RAMROD
Charles N. Heckelmann

Most men would have cut their losses, but Frazer counted the bullets in his guns and said he'd soak the range in blood before he'd give up another inch of what was his.

LONE GUN
Eric Allen

Smoke Blackbird had been away too long. The Lequires had seized the Blackbird farm, forcing the Indians and settlers off, and no one seemed willing to fight! He had to fight alone.

THE THIRD RIDER
Barry Cord

Mel Rawlins wasn't going to let anything stand in his way. His father was murdered, his two brothers gone. Now Mel rode for vengeance.

ARIZONA DRIFTERS
W. C. Tuttle

When drifting Dutton and Lonnie Steelman decide to become partners they find that they have a common enemy in the formidable Thurston brothers.

TOMBSTONE
Matt Braun

Wells Fargo paid Luke Starbuck to outgun the silver-thieving stagecoach gang at Tombstone. Before long Luke can see the only thing bearing fruit in this eldorado will be the gallows tree.

HIGH BORDER RIDERS
Lee Floren

Buckshot McKee and Tortilla Joe cut the trail of a border tough who was running Mexican beef into Texas. They stopped the smuggler in his tracks.

BRETT RANDALL, GAMBLER
E. B. Mann

Larry Day had the choice of running away from the law or of assuming a dead man's place. No matter what he decided he was bound to end up dead.

THE GUNSHARP
William R. Cox

The Eggerleys weren't very smart. They trained their sights on Will Carney and Arizona's biggest blood bath began.

THE DEPUTY OF SAN RIANO
Lawrence A. Keating and
Al. P. Nelson

When a man fell dead from his horse, Ed Grant was spotted riding away from the scene. The deputy sheriff rode out after him and came up against everything from gunfire to dynamite.

FARGO: MASSACRE RIVER
John Benteen

The ambushers up ahead had now blocked the road. Fargo's convoy was a jumble, a perfect target for the insurgents' weapons!

SUNDANCE: DEATH IN THE LAVA
John Benteen

The Modoc's captured the wagon train and its cargo of gold. But now the halfbreed they called Sundance was going after it . . .

HARSH RECKONING
Phil Ketchum

Five years of keeping himself alive in a brutal prison had made Brand tough and careless about who he gunned down . . .

FARGO: PANAMA GOLD
John Benteen

With foreign money behind him, Buckner was going to destroy the Panama Canal before it could be completed. Fargo's job was to stop Buckner.

FARGO:
THE SHARPSHOOTERS
John Benteen

The Canfield clan, thirty strong were raising hell in Texas. Fargo was tough enough to hold his own against the whole clan.

PISTOL LAW
Paul Evan Lehman

Lance Jones came back to Mustang for just one thing — revenge! Revenge on the people who had him thrown in jail.

HELL RIDERS
Steve Mensing

Wade Walker's kid brother, Duane, was locked up in the Silver City jail facing a rope at dawn. Wade was a ruthless outlaw, but he was smart, and he had vowed to have his brother out of jail before morning!

DESERT OF THE DAMNED
Nelson Nye

The law was after him for the murder of a marshal — a murder he didn't commit. Breen was after him for revenge — and Breen wouldn't stop at anything . . . blackmail, a frameup . . . or murder.

DAY OF THE COMANCHEROS
Steven C. Lawrence

Their very name struck terror into men's hearts — the Comancheros, a savage army of cutthroats who swept across Texas, leaving behind a bloodstained trail of robbery and murder.